OUTREACH

Date Due

1/4/99	MAY 04 2000		
FE 9 '00	SEP 1 2 '00		
MR 15 '99	10-17-00		
AP 14 '99	FEB 1 3 '0		
MAY 2 4 '99	MAY 17 0		
JY 19 '99	OC 15 05		
AG 19 '99	9-12-05		
OCT 1 0 199	OCT 1 2 '06		
DEC 29 1999			
MR 8			
APR 26 2000			

12/98

Jackson
   County
      Library
         Services

HEADQUARTERS
413 W.Main
Medford, Oregon 97501

D1443047

MALICE DOMESTIC

MALICE DOMESTIC

Rae Foley

G.K. Hall & Co.   •   Chivers Press
Thorndike, Maine USA   Bath, England

JACKSON COUNTY LIBRARY SERVICES
MEDFORD OREGON 97501

This Large Print edition is published by G.K. Hall & Co., USA
and by Chivers Press, England.

Published in 1998 in the U.S. by arrangement
with Golden West Literary Agency.

Published in 1999 in the U.K. by arrangement
with Golden West Literary Agency.

U.S. Hardcover 0-7838-0385-0 (Romance Series Edition)
U.K. Hardcover 0-7540-3569-7 (Chivers Large Print)
U.K. Softcover 0-7540-3570-0 (Camden Large Print)

The text of this Large Print edition is unabridged.
Other aspects of the book may vary from the original edition.

Set in 16 pt. Plantin by Minnie B. Raven.

Printed in the United States on permanent paper.

British Library Cataloguing in Publication Data available

Library of Congress Cataloging in Publication Data

Foley, Rae 1900–
    Malice domestic / Rae Foley.
      p. cm.
    ISBN 0-7838-0385-0 (lg. print : hc : alk. paper)
    1. Large type books.   I. Title.
[PS3511.O186M35   1998]
  813′.54—dc21   98-41390

**For Sybil
incomparable sister**

1

There were two schools of thought about Barry Hamilton. According to one of them he was a crusader dedicated to revealing the truth. Even if someone got hurt, and in the course of his exposés someone inevitably got hurt, it was all in a good cause. Truth must be served and the public must be informed.

The other school of thought maintained simply that the man was a rat who destroyed reputations out of a malignant combination of malice and envy. I had never met him but I joined the second group automatically. All I had to go on was the fact that Paula had married him. Paula was my sister, six years older than I. I adored her, but she had a blind spot about men. In the ten years before she was thirty she had married twice and both of the men she fell for were phony.

Barry was a great one for informing the public. Once he had chosen a subject — or a victim — for a book, he set to work like a doctor performing an autopsy to dissect the man, to cut him down to size, to nose out any peccadilloes and reveal them with astonished horror as though no one had ever be-

7

fore had a human weakness. A drunken party at college became an orgy. An early affair with a perfectly willing girl suggested the act of a monster of vice. Membership in the Parent-Teachers Association looked like affiliation with the fascist party.

He escaped libel suits by the skin of his teeth. Partisans of his victims wrote enraged letters to the editors of newspapers. Occasionally he received anonymous threats of which he informed the press, squeezing the last ounce of publicity juice out of them. And he sold and sold. Even people who hated his guts bought his books, partly — and I admit this with the utmost reluctance as I loathe giving the man a fair break — because he wrote brilliantly; partly because he appealed to the universal Peeping Tom. Whether you admired Barry Hamilton or foamed at the mouth when his name was mentioned, you read him as an act of self-protection. Otherwise you didn't know what everyone else was talking about.

When Barry picked as the subject of his next book Eliot Masters, the good-looking young governor who was well ahead of the field as a popular contender for the presidency, many people thought he had gone too far. Rumors spread like a brush fire, but Barry, smiling his Mona Lisa smile, refused to comment beyond declaring that he was finding the material "unexpected and a challenge."

Everyone read what he wanted to into that statement except Eliot Masters himself. In television appearances the Governor became more and more strained. He looked hagridden. Like Barry he had no comment to make on the forthcoming book beyond saying that he shared the public's admiration for Mr. Hamilton's fine writing and his "sense of fair play." Though he kept his hands in his pockets while he made the statement, I knew he must have his fingers crossed.

From all I could make out, Paula had taken one look at Barry Hamilton and gone down for the count. It's hard to explain about Paula. At thirty she looked not much more than seventeen. She was beautiful and, partly because she was so small, partly because of a misleading air of helplessness, she gave people the impression of an angora kitten, adorable, a plaything, somewhat silly. Actually, behind that childish appearance there was a doctorate in philosophy, a skilled pilot, and a demon editor with a relentless eye for sloppy writing.

Men had been falling in love with Paula since she was sixteen, men who would have cherished her, who longed to take care of her. And yet she had married twice, men who were completely self-centered, who demanded uncritical admiration and devotion, and who actually abused her. When, long after everyone else, she saw the manner of man

9

she had married, she broke away quickly and got a divorce. For a woman who wore blinders where men were concerned, she took swift action once disillusionment came.

Something complex and confused in Paula behind that radiant beauty and her essential sweetness seemed to seek out punishment — unhappiness instead of happiness, unkindness instead of kindness. The psychiatrists probably have a neat term for it. So when she wrote that she had fallen in love with Barry Hamilton, the best-selling author on the Webb Publishing Company list and that she was going to marry him, I wondered how much more punishment she could take and how long this marriage would last.

It lasted three months. It ended when someone cracked Barry Hamilton's skull with a piece of lead pipe. A few hours later, Paula was found drowned in their swimming pool. The newspapers, the police who investigated, the Hamilton family themselves, all said suicide.

I said murder.

II

I said it to Joe Maitland who had drifted around to find out how the rehearsals were going. At least, that's what he told me. I didn't appear in the second act so I had slipped out

10

of the barn, which had been turned into a summer stock theater, and sat on a cushion on the ground, grateful to rest as I was still recuperating. Joe had provided the cushion. He sat on the grass beside me, his hands clasped around his drawn-up knees, a pipe in his mouth, wiry red hair standing on end, his homely freckled face looking sleepy. As usual, his stocky body was arrayed in shabby slacks, a worn sweater, and scuffed shoes. As usual, too, the car he had parked in the lot behind the barn was a dilapidated heap.

He was no Cary Grant but he had steady brown eyes and a kind mouth. As a rule he was the most reasonable person I know, though he could be stubborn, too; for instance, he had really dug in his heels about going into the family business and fitting into the plans they had made for him, but even then he was good-natured about it.

"I am not pigheaded, Sarah Bernhardt," he told me placidly, "just firm. Unlike the majority of mankind I know exactly what I want."

What he wanted most was me. He had been proposing to me at intervals for three years and taking me out gratefully when nothing better offered. There was no one on earth of whom I was fonder, except for Paula, of course, but no one could be romantic about Joe. He was wasting his time with me and I told him so about once a week.

11

There was never any misunderstanding between us on that score.

"I can't decide whether I'm a lapdog or a watchdog," he said once. "Anyhow, I'm gambling on the idea that you'll get so used to having me around that you won't be able to do without me."

The nicest thing about Joe was that he really listened. He listened now, puffing ruminatively at his pipe, while I told him why I believed Paula had been murdered. I had truly loved her, though we had seen little of each other in the eight years since she had gone to New York after her first disastrous marriage. But I could hear in my own voice, for all my genuine grief, that I was dramatizing the situation, though if murder isn't dramatic I don't know what is.

It was typical of Joe that his first reaction was to produce a clean white handkerchief — however shabby his clothes might be, his linen was always impeccable — hold it to my nose and say, "Blow, Baby."

I blew. Then I wiped my nose and eyes. Crying hadn't improved my looks but Joe never seemed to mind about that either. No one had ever believed Paula and I were sisters. She was blonde and beautiful. I am dark, hair and eyes and skin, with a kind of gypsy coloring, and I'm not beautiful. Even Joe never claimed that I was. "It's not a bad face," he would say in one of his more expansive moments, "but then I'm used to it."

Now he was silent for a long time. At last he said, "Some people are fated for disaster. I always felt that Paula was one of them. She might have been the apple of her husband's eye. Instead, she always got hurt. In a sense, she asked for it."

I sniffed. "I know. When she said she had married Barry I thought, 'Here we go again.'"

"What happened, anyhow?" As I started to speak he waggled his pipe at me warningly. "Don't try to write the script, Eleanora Duse. Just tell me what you know."

After her second divorce, Paula had started working for the Webb Publishing Company, beginning as a reader and working up to assistant editor. The day before, I had dug out all her letters and reread them so the story was clear enough in my mind. She had liked her job, she had liked her associates, she had especially liked Dexter Webb, head of the company. In fact, there had been a time when I half expected him to be Number Three, because, for Paula, there always had to be someone she could adore.

When I asked her if this wasn't the house that published Barry Hamilton, she answered rather defensively that, after all, publishers were businessmen and had to show a profit. Almost every house had someone like Hamilton whose huge sales made it possible for them to publish really good books that

13

wouldn't pay off so well.

Then, four months earlier, she was told that she was to edit the new Hamilton book and she met the author.

"Absolutely charming," she wrote, "and completely sincere. All the terrible stories we've heard must have been started by people who were jealous or whom he had exposed."

A month after that, she telephoned long distance, breathless with happiness, to say she and Barry had just got married privately. They would have a weekend honeymoon and then break the news to the family.

"Those were her exact words? Break the news?" Joe asked.

"Paula explained about that later. Barry was the sole support of his family: father, mother, sister, and brother. No, I'm wrong about the brother. He is married to a rich woman."

Joe grunted. He is allergic to men who are supported by women, whether financially or emotionally. He has always contended that the more a man depends on a woman to build his ego the louder masculine noises he has to make. Joe doesn't like noisy people.

"Anyhow, Paula moved out to the Hamilton house in Connecticut but she kept on with her job."

"Why?" As Joe pointed out, Paula was no career girl. In the past she had worked because she had no money of her own and she refused alimony. No one could say that Hamilton was not in the chips. He could afford to support a wife. And what Paula really wanted was to devote herself to some man. Immolate herself.

"Immolate! Now who's being dramatic?" I scoffed. But it was true in a way. "I thought Paula thought the Hamiltons thought —"

"Hey," Joe protested.

I started over. "Well, Barry was already supporting his family, paying all the expenses of the house. I guess he — or maybe Paula herself — didn't want them to resent her as an extra expense or something."

"Now that would be just too damned bad. And what kind of character was Hamilton that he would let his wife be an intruder in his own house?"

"I don't know. Paula thought he was wonderful, brilliant, burning with a hard, gemlike flame."

"She always did go overboard." Joe added gently, "Poor Paula," and I started to cry again. "What did she think of her in-laws?"

"She didn't say much except that they seemed to be very nice."

"So I take it she didn't like them."

"Well, it seems to be quite an odd household. Even Barry's ex-fiancée lives there."

"Well!" Joe looked at me, his brown eyes as round as doughnuts. "It's a wonder to me

15

someone didn't take a club to that guy." And then he fell silent for that is exactly what someone had done.

Barry Hamilton, as headlines and news commentators proclaimed far and wide, had been found at the desk in his study, his skull crushed, a piece of lead pipe on the floor beside his body. The reason for the headlines was that the finished script of his book on Eliot Masters, leading contender for the presidency, had disappeared.

And that, as Joe said somberly, put the lid on Eliot Masters' chances. His political career was as dead as the dodo. Even now, still shocked by Barry's murder, heartsick and bereft by Paula's death, I was dimly aware that the real tragedy was Masters', or perhaps the country's. Masters had represented youth and hope, confidence and courage. All that was ended. Whether he had any guilty knowledge of Barry's murder and the disappearance of the book did not matter. Barry had been killed to suppress the book and whatever it had to reveal about Masters. That was what counted. Not even his most faithful supporters would dare consider his candidacy now.

Joe knocked out his pipe and looked around as voices called from the barn. They had finished the run-through of the second act and were taking a ten-minute break. I got up and brushed off my slacks.

"I'm on at the beginning of the third act."

16

Actually I had only three lines and I wasn't on the stage more than twenty minutes during the whole play. With a company that size they would normally have doubled the part or cut it altogether. As Joe financed the theater I suspected that the fact I had it was his doing but he would never admit it. Lousy as I was, if I wanted to be an actress he would help me to be an actress.

All he said now was, "Okay, Sarah Siddons, I'll be waiting," and he settled himself once more on the grass, stretching out as though he were going to sleep, but his round eyes were wide open and he was frowning.

When I had spoken my final, deathless line, "I'll give him the message on my way home, Mrs. Blake," I found Joe still lying on his back, staring at the sky. He got up quickly when he saw me. "Come on, I'm starving. Let's go to Mack's."

Mack had a hotdog stand not far from the theater. Joe came out carefully balancing two hotdogs lavishly spread with mustard and two bottles of beer. When we had finished that elegant repast and wiped off the last of the mustard, Joe dropped the bottles in a trash basket, gave me a cigarette, lighted it, and filled his pipe.

Without consulting me he drove back through town to his own house. Where the driveway ended, we walked through the famous rose gardens and out into the woods.

17

There were a couple of canvas chairs into one of which Joe collapsed.

"Sometimes," I said severely, "it seems to me you spend your whole life just lounging around."

"I have never seen much point in feverish activity. Consider the ant. There's a horrible warning for you of the futility of busyness for its own sake. I've watched an ant strain its guts out hauling something twice its size the length of our terrace, and then forget all about it and start on something else that is equally silly."

His lazy voice didn't change at all. "Sue, why do you think Paula was murdered?"

"She called me after Barry was found. That was the day I got the attack of acute appendicitis. I was feverish and in pain and I didn't know what was wrong with me, and I was trying to understand her. She was horribly shocked, of course, as anyone is by a senseless act of violence and brutality, but she wasn't suicidal. She was trying desperately to tell me something. She said, 'I hate to do this to you, Sue, but I know you won't let me down,' or 'You're the only one who won't let me down.' I'm not sure which. And she said, 'I know you'll understand my message. I've put it . . . Who's that?' in a startled way and broke the connection. And then she died. But — no one even told me she was dead, Joe. That was the cruelest thing. I don't understand the Hamiltons. They must have known I was her only family and how close we were. Anyhow, I heard it next day on the radio at the hospital: 'Barry Hamilton's widow a suicide,' they said."

"Yes, I heard that one in California."

I asked suspiciously, "Is that why you flew back here so unexpectedly?"

Joe looked at me, looked down at his scuffed shoes. "Sure. I thought I might come in handy."

"Oh, Joe!"

"Think nothing of it. So you heard the broadcast —"

"I'd had an emergency operation the night before. When they wouldn't let me leave the hospital I just about went out of my mind. I got to a telephone somehow and called the Hamilton house in Connecticut. It seemed to take hours. Finally I got someone, a woman with a voice like soft custard, who said, 'Paula's sister? Oh — well — I suppose you had better talk to her lawyer.' "

Joe was grinning. When he became aware of it he apologized. "I can't help it, Sue. You may not be Maude Adams but you are the best imitator I ever came across. I could hear that woman's gluey voice. And what about the lawyer?"

"I was stunned. I felt as though the woman had slapped my face, and Paula was dead and people were saying she had killed herself.

19

Well, the nurses got me back to bed and there were complications, one thing and another. Not very interesting but they prevented me from attending the funeral. Actually, it was three days before I could even get to a telephone again and call the lawyer. Luckily I remembered his name, Warren King, because Paula had mentioned him occasionally as a friend of the family. He seemed to be there quite a lot. I told him I was Paula's sister. He didn't like me either."

"Either? Oh, you mean Old Glue."

"Yes. He said no one had known my address so they had been unable to reach me, but naturally he had been expecting my call."

Joe's sandy eyebrows shot up. "Her lawyer had been expecting your call? What gives?" He reached out to open my clenched fist, finger by finger, and hold it lightly in his own.

"He said a rather peculiar and disturbing situation had arisen. At the time of their marriage, he had drawn up wills for Barry and Paula in which they left everything to each other. The day before her death, as of course she must have informed me, Paula had changed her will, making me her sole beneficiary."

Joe expelled a long breath. "Well, well!"

"So I told him that Paula had not informed me but that she had nothing to leave except what had been her husband's and I

20

didn't feel entitled to that. He was kind of surprised."

Joe laughed. "Naturally. About all you and Paula had in common was a complete lack of any sense of self-preservation where money is concerned."

"He seemed to be relieved. He said he felt I was taking the proper attitude. In any case, there might be some question as to the validity of the second will. The verdict at the inquest had been suicide while of unsound mind and Paula had been — well, not herself — for some days before she killed herself."

Joe sat bolt upright, which is no small feat on a canvas lawn chair. "The lawyer said that?" He was dumfounded. "He wanted to upset Paula's will?"

I nodded emphatically. "And he said," my voice began to shake and Joe's grip on my hand tightened, "he said the services for Paula and Barry had been held that morning. Fortunately there had been a minimum of speculation about Paula's suicide as the personal tragedy had been submerged in the national scandal involving Eliot Masters. Mr. King said he was glad for my sake I had been spared the ordeal of the funeral, particularly as the Hamiltons were shattered by the double tragedy and the terrific uproar in the press. He said when the legal details were straightened out he would send me the proper papers to sign so Paula's estate — or

21

rather, Barry Hamilton's estate — could be restored to his family. And he congratulated me on this act of justice."

After a long time Joe said, "And just why did you tamely accept the lawyer's orders and go back, as of today, to your dazzling triumph in the Lenox Stock Company?"

"Well, in the first place, I didn't want Barry's money, and that's what it amounts to. In all fairness, I thought it should belong to his family. After all, he was the one who earned it."

"And in the second place?"

"I was afraid," I said bluntly. "Something is awfully wrong, Joe. Paula tried to tell me something and she was murdered just as surely as Barry was murdered."

"But why?"

"I think she knew who killed Barry and the murderer believes that she told me. In fact, I think she did tell me if I could only find her message."

2

It was Joe who, over my feverish protests, insisted that I give up my bit part with the Lenox group and go to Stockford. If Barry's murderer thought I had any inkling as to his identity, my only safety lay in exposing him before he found me. And if Paula had left some clue to the killer, we were going to dig it up if we had to tear all of Stockford apart.

I fought with every argument I could muster. I didn't want the money. I didn't like the Hamiltons. I couldn't bring Paula back. I was afraid. I might as well have talked to an empty theater. Joe had dug in his heels.

"What do you want me to do," I asked bitterly, "aside from setting me up as bait for a murderer?"

"This is one murderer I'd like to track straight to hell. I could do without Hamilton who spent his life spoiling other lives and made a small fortune out of it. But Paula was different. She was lovely and sweet and she never hurt anyone. And there's you — for what you're worth, wench. And then," he hesitated, "there's Eliot Masters who might have become a great president, and think

23

how few there have been. Four? Five, perhaps? No, we are going to wrap this little joker up in cellophane and present him with our compliments to the police. It would be rather pleasant to give Masters back to his country with all the mud scraped off."

"Considering that the press of the world is screaming, and the two major parties are hurling hysterical and irresponsible charges and countercharges at each other, it seems likely the police aren't missing any bets. What do you think Joe Maitland can do that they aren't doing?"

"Look where they aren't looking," Joe said, and he refused to add to that.

As luck would have it we made the three hundred mile run from Pennsylvania to Connecticut on one of the hottest days of the summer. Joe, as usual, was driving a heap so there was no air conditioning. We sweltered but we didn't talk much.

Once Joe said, "We'll play it cool. Remember, Sue, if this setup should be what it appears to be, murder to prevent publication of the Masters book, we're playing in the big league."

"What it appears to be?" As Joe had given me only twenty-four hours' notice of the trip to Stockford, probably to forestall any further arguments on my side, I had spent Sunday getting clothes in order, packing, writing notes, and explaining to the producer of the

24

Lenox group that I'd have to withdraw from the cast. I must say he accepted this news with cheerful equanimity.

Now I had the great bulk of the unread Sunday *Times* on my lap. There was no escaping the Hamilton murder. After a glance at the first page, MASTERS MAY WITHDRAW FROM PRIMARY, I turned to the News of the Week, where there was a recapitulation of the effect of the scandal on the forthcoming election. The Book Review was no help. The first page contained two articles, pro and con, on Barry Hamilton and his fabulous career as a biographer. One made some carefully phrased references to the Manchester book and a writer's freedom to bring out all the facts. It stressed Hamilton's enormous sales, his brilliant writing, his vivid reporting. The other took the sturdy stand that Hamilton's books had destroyed careers, wrecked reputations, left his subjects too often victims of innuendoes as destructive as any spread by the late Senator McCarthy. *De mortuis* and all that, but a writer was supposed to have ethics as well as ability.

Even the Magazine Section devoted an article to Barry Hamilton, a profile signed by his publisher, Dexter Webb. There was a full-length picture at which I looked for a long time. This was the man whom Paula had loved. This was the man whom someone had hated enough to bash over the head. That

25

took a lot of hate. Other pictures had been carefully posed, showing Barry at his desk against an impressive background of leather-bound books, one hand idly resting on what was presumably his current bombshell, the famous Mona Lisa smile on his lips. This was a candid camera shot taken, according to the credit line, by Mrs. Sarah Oliphant.

In the full-length picture I saw something of the quality Paula had fallen in love with. His hands were in the pockets of his slacks, his head was flung back, and he was laughing. Even just looking at the picture you wanted to laugh back. I turned the page and caught my breath, Paula was there, her enchanting face lighted by her lovely smile. Dexter Webb had quoted a Jacobean epitaph:

He first deceased; she for a little tried
To live without him, liked it not, and died.

"But it isn't true," I protested. "It didn't happen like that; I don't believe it."

"Put away the paper. It will only upset you. Anyhow, all these wise guys simply add to the confusion. And I do wish you'd move that damned suitcase of yours. When it isn't whacking my leg it's on the gears."

I moved my offending handbag with a jerk and, as it was the kind with two open pockets, I managed to spill compact, lipstick, and doorkey onto the floor of the car.

"You know, Joe, this is going to be awfully awkward, isn't it? The Hamiltons don't want to see me, and I don't think the lawyer is going to like it much either."

"Something stinks to high heaven about that lawyer, Sue. For my money he smells like the Jersey flats and I can't say more. I think we're going to stir up the animals." He took his hand off the wheel to lay it on mine, which is about as far as his passionate love-making ever got. "But, remember you aren't being thrust into the tiger's cage. Papa will keep an eye on you."

"Papa had better," I said grimly.

At three thirty we reached Stockford, Connecticut. In winter this was a sleepy New England village of 5,000 inhabitants. By midsummer it became a thriving resort town of 20,000. Some of the summer people rented cottages on the lakes or furnished rooms in the village, on whose profits the thrifty New Englanders lived until the following summer. Most of the vacationers drifted in and out, staying in the motels that cluttered the highways while they participated in or attended the summer theater, symphony concerts, chamber music, ballet, and the art exhibits that pop up all over New England like measles. It seems to me that everyone in Connecticut who isn't writing books is painting pictures.

There was a single vacancy at the Stockford Inn, and for that one night only,

27

which Joe got for me. He is a man who never gives up and he had no intention of leaving me there alone, so he ignored the clerk's assurance that there wasn't another bed available. I wasn't surprised when, after a long talk over the counter, the desk clerk discovered a small attic room. It would be hot and uncomfortable, he said discouragingly. The window was low; there were no furnishings beyond a single bed, a sewing machine, and a table. The room was used for sorting and mending linen.

"That will be fine," Joe said cheerfully.

"Everything is taken for the rest of the season. We have reservations for weeks," the clerk warned him.

"Something is bound to turn up. We'll worry about that when the time comes." When the bellboy took my bag, Joe said, "Don't spend too much time changing. I want to see that so-called lawyer before his office closes."

Mine not to reason why. I put on a thin white dress with a black belt — the closest thing I had to mourning, but I knew Paula had always disliked outward displays of grief — and went down to find Joe waiting for me in the lobby. For once he was as presentable as his English tailor could make him, though he flatly refused to control his red hair with any kind of grease, however sexily it might be advertised.

28

Warren King had a two-room office suite just off Main Street, up a dusty flight of stairs and above a specialty food shop. The middle-aged woman clerk in the outer office gaped when I gave her my name and hastily shut the door of the inner office behind her. I could hear an agitated whisper.

Mr. King did not bother to come out to greet me. The clerk held open the door while I went in followed by Joe. I thought she closed it rather reluctantly. After all, I was, if remotely, part of the Great Scandal.

The lawyer was a fairly tall man in his early forties, moderately good looking, with a receding hairline and an advancing stomach. His hands were soft and his handshake like grasping a moist rubber glove. I was aware of his eyes weighing us both while he offered that limp handshake and two hard chairs. When he sat down in his deep upholstered chair behind his desk I had a curious feeling that he had barricaded himself against us. Which, of course, was absurd.

It took about half a minute in the lawyer's presence to confirm the impression I'd got over the telephone. He didn't like me at all.

"Well, Miss Wales, this is an unexpected — that is, I understood that you would not be coming to Stockford at this time. The Hamiltons have sustained a considerable shock."

"So," Joe put in mildly, "has Miss Wales.

29

Her sister was very dear to her."

"I take it, Mr. — Um, you represent Miss Wales's interests."

"I'm not a lawyer, if that's what you mean, but I do represent Miss Wales's interests. By the way, whose interests do you represent, Mr. King?"

"I was Mrs. Barry Hamilton's lawyer. At least I drew up her will." He corrected himself. "Wills."

"As I understand it," Joe said, "you are encouraging Miss Wales to disregard your client's wishes and give up her inheritance. I suppose it's a fairly substantial one."

King pressed his lips together tightly. At last he capitulated. "You might say so."

"If Miss Wales does not accept it, who would inherit? The Hamilton family?"

"I gather that you have persuaded Miss Wales to change her mind about that." The lawyer smiled nastily. "Whose interests are you representing, Mr. Um?"

I was so furious that I forgot Joe's warning about playing it cool. "Look here," I sputtered, "if you think for one single minute he is trying to make money out of me you're out of your mind. He is Joseph Wentworth Maitland."

King looked at me as though he had been poked in the solar plexus. There are only half a dozen family fortunes bigger than the Maitlands' in this country, and the Went-

30

worths run them a close second. It's quite a combination.

"I'm sorry if I have given you the wrong impression, Mr. Maitland." If I hadn't disliked the man before, the abject apology in his voice would have done the trick. He sat looking at Joe as though he expected currency to sprout on his jacket and gold certificates to drop from his lips.

"You didn't," Joe said pleasantly. He looked at his watch. "We won't take up more of your time this afternoon. We just wanted to spare you any unnecessary legal work until we have an opportunity to explore the situation."

King ran a finger under his collar. "Are you planning to stay in Stockford long, Mr. Maitland?" By this time, he had practically forgotten that I was there.

"Indefinitely," Joe said in a definite tone before I could speak. "There are so many things to clear up, aren't there? But first, of course, we would like to meet the Hamiltons. Perhaps this evening."

"They are completely in seclusion. They have not only suffered a deep personal loss in Barry's tragic death," King saw my angry eyes and added hastily, "and Mrs. Hamilton's, of course, but they have been driven mad by reporters. They are living in a state of siege. The inexplicable disappearance of the Masters script has brought newsmen

31

from everywhere. The situation is a nightmare. The whole country seems to be hounding them."

"The whole country is involved in the next presidential election," Joe pointed out. "I'm afraid the Hamiltons will have to take second place to the public interest. And Miss Wales naturally wants to know more about her sister's death." He was smiling but it was obvious that nothing under heaven would move him. Like the postman he would follow his appointed round. Regardless.

The lawyer gave up. "I'll get in touch with them. Prepare them." Seeing Joe's expression he added defensively, "Let me point out that the Hamiltons are the least grasping people I have ever encountered, completely unworldly. But if Miss Wales has changed her mind, you can hardly blame them for feeling some resentment if an utter stranger, a woman whom he never saw in his life, inherits Barry's entire fortune. They simply won't know where to turn. They were dependent on him for everything they had."

"Why were they?" Joe sounded interested but not sympathetic. "Anything wrong with them that they couldn't support themselves?"

King's mouth opened and closed. I think he was relieved when the telephone rang. He spoke curtly and then his voice changed. "Ruth!" He glanced at us. "I'll call you back. Some clients —"

"Be seeing you." Joe caught my eye and I got up.

King covered the mouthpiece. "What are your plans?"

"We'll keep you informed. We'll be around." Joe stood back so I could go through the clerk's office. My big handbag snagged on the edge of her desk with the usual result. While Joe scrabbled around, picking things up, I heard the lawyer say in a low voice, "Ruth, something unexpected has happened. I'm on my way."

3

The inn served drinks at little tables scattered over the lawn under wineglass elms and maples. The day had been swelteringly, blisteringly hot, the thermometer hovering around the ninety degree mark, but in the shade of the great trees there was a fresh breeze. We lingered over long frosted rum collinses and cooled off.

Joe, who had been talking a blue streak of lighthearted nonsense designed to cheer the patient, broke off abruptly. "You haven't heard a word I've been saying."

"I've been thinking. There's something up your sleeve, isn't there?"

Joe ordered another round of drinks. "Did anything about that meeting with King strike you as odd?"

"Well, aside from the fact that he hates my guts —"

"Indelicately expressed, but I'll concede you are his least favorite character."

"And I'll bet I know why. You remember the telephone call from Ruth? That's the name of Barry's sister, and I gathered from Paula that she and King are as thick as thieves."

"Not a tactful comment. You're going to have to watch that tongue of yours, Sue. Still I do see what you mean. How much grieving the Hamiltons are doing over the dear departed I don't know, but it's clear that King is grieving over that lost estate, particularly if he'd like a slice of it himself."

"Well, to be fair about it, I must say I think they are justified, Joe."

"Which brings us back to the question: Why did Paula change her will? And another point strikes me with a dull thud."

"Points can't do that."

"This one can. Would King ever have divulged the existence of that second will if he hadn't assumed that you already knew of it from Paula? We keep coming back to the fact that there had to be a reason, something powerful enough to make Paula set aside the Hamilton claims."

"And yet, if you stop to think about it, Barry himself didn't seem to have given their claims much weight. He gave the works to Paula and cut them right out."

"Of course, anyone knowing Paula would have been sure she would cut them right back in."

"Except," I pointed out, "that she didn't." So we had come full circle.

The waiter announced that our table was ready and we sat down to the best lobster I'd ever tasted outside Maine. Eating lobster requires a certain single-mindedness so it was some time before the waiter removed our bibs and we settled back for coffee and brandy. For the moment I was replete and content.

"I'll say one thing for you, Sue. When you eat you give it your full attention."

"Miss Sue Wales?" The man beside our table was tall and lanky, with a careless sort of charm of which he seemed to be completely unaware. "I am Dexter Webb."

When I had introduced Joe, the latter signaled the waiter for another chair, coffee, and brandy.

"You aren't at all like Paula, are you?" the publisher said.

I shook my head, fought back the silly tears. "Not at all."

"In a way I am almost glad. I was rather dreading a resemblance." Then he said quietly, as though he were giving me time to regain control, "I came here because I felt there should be someone to tell you, 'I'm sorry.'" He added, "Sorrier than I can say." He went on almost angrily. "What can anyone say when someone young and beautiful and sweet just — goes out? She should have had another thirty or forty years. It makes you think of that terrible line of Webster's: 'Cover her face; mine eyes dazzle; she died young.'"

"You knew her a long time, didn't you?"

36

"About four years." His face lighted in an amused smile. "You know the funny thing is that I hired her in the first place because she was so incredibly decorative to have around. When I discovered that she was a natural-born editor it seemed almost too much. She — I can't imagine the office without her; I'd come to depend on her so completely." He broke off.

"You know," I told him, "before she married Barry I had a kind of idea, from the way she wrote, that it might be you."

"No, I was never in the running. Paula made that clear from the beginning. Good friends, yes. Marriage, no. I didn't have whatever it was she wanted in a man." He tried to speak lightly but I heard the pain in his voice and knew that he had loved her. "It was Barry from the beginning, Barry to the very end."

Before I could speak Joe interposed, "How did you know we were here?"

Dexter leaned back in his chair and again his face revealed amusement. "I heard it from the Hamiltons. Barry lent me his guest-house for weekends. Now — normally I wouldn't be here on a Monday but I've stayed on to go through Barry's files and see whether I can find carbon copies of the Masters book."

"You'd publish it?"

"Would I!" The pleasant face held a grim

look. "If I can find it I'll get it out so fast the Masters group won't know what hit them."

"If they were back of Hamilton's murder won't you be taking a risk?"

"You don't think that would stop me?" The publisher sounded incredulous.

"That's right. You're personally involved in this mess, aren't you?"

"Involved! My best friend, my best author, my best book, my best source of income, my best editor — all gone in a flash."

Joe has the irritating insistence of a leaky tap. "You say the Hamiltons told you we were here?"

"Actually, it was Luella Matthews." As we both looked a question Dexter explained, "She was once engaged to Barry. She just — ah — stayed on after he broke the engagement and married Paula."

"Well, well," Joe said mildly.

Dexter smiled. "I know how it sounds, but the Hamiltons are an odd sort of family. Right now they are in a tizzy because Warren King came rushing out to tell Ruth — that's Barry's sister — Miss Wales had arrived and had decided to claim Barry's estate, after all."

"After all what?" Joe asked.

Dexter chuckled. "After all their hopes had been raised."

"But the estate," Joe said, "was Paula's."

"There seems to be some legal question

about the validity of Paula's second will. She wasn't — herself — for several days before her suicide. And the verdict, 'unsound mind,' is a strong weapon for the Hamiltons."

"In other words," Joe said, again before I could speak, "the Hamiltons intend to fight."

"They would never express it like that." Dexter looked amused. "They would be more likely to talk of justice and fair play and Paula's mental condition but, in a refined sort of way, they are leeches. They're the kind of people who accept money absent-mindedly as though they weren't aware of what they were doing."

Joe grinned. "You don't like them either."

"Either?" Dexter was quick. "You mean Paula didn't like them? I wouldn't have guessed that, though, of course, the Hamiltons made clear that they were deeply disappointed when Barry more or less jilted Luella. But Paula's manners were so invariably gentle, so . . ." He stopped and lifted his brandy glass with an unsteady hand. "In any case, don't let them get you down, Miss Wales."

"Somehow I dread meeting them."

He laughed and his eyes narrowed to show just a glint of mirth. "Right now, they are a lot more scared than you are. They are trembling in their boots while they wait for you to walk in. I guaranteed to deliver you."

"Scared of me?" I was incredulous.

39

"Actually, of your companion. When Warren said you were accompanied by Maitland who obviously was going to look after your interests, they felt as though you had brought an H bomb to fight a brush fire, that they were outclassed." He laughed again.

I looked at Joe in surprise. It was always difficult to remember that this unimpressive character packed a lot of weight. I will say for him that he never threw it around.

"Who are these people?" he asked. "What are they like?"

"Well, now." Dexter considered them, frowning. "Barry's father and mother, of course. Pleasant enough but just so damned negative that I can't describe them at all. Then there is Barry's sister Ruth who lives in a state of self-imposed martyrdom. I think she has got to the point where she believes in it herself."

"Is she the one King plans to marry?" Joe asked.

This time Dexter considered more carefully. "Let's put it this way. So far he hasn't got around to committing himself."

"But he might — if she got part of her brother's estate?"

Dexter grinned. "Oh, look here, what do you expect me to say to that?"

Joe grinned back. "Just what you have said."

"Then we come to Tommy." Dexter spoke

40

without enthusiasm. "He's Barry's younger brother, the baby of the family."

"How young?"

"Thirty-four, I think."

"And still Tommy?"

"Now and always the boyish type. Married to a woman twelve years his senior. Blanche has an income of thirty thousand a year." Dexter came to a full halt.

"And this Luella — what was she doing at the house after Barry brought home a wife? What kind of girl would accept a situation like that?"

"After all, Maitland, it was a home, her living costs her nothing, and the Hamiltons are fond of her." Dexter had a lopsided smile. "I'm afraid the presence of Joseph Wentworth Maitland will shatter what little composure the Hamiltons have managed to collect. I'll beard the lion's den with you, Miss Wales." He looked at Joe, brows raised in a question. "If that's all right with you."

"Oh, sure. Just bring her back alive."

II

The car into which Dexter helped me was a stunning new Chrysler.

"It's Barry's," he explained. "You know, Miss Wales, not until after Barry's murder did I realize how dependent we all were on

41

him." He saw my surprise. "Oh, yes, I was, too. The Webb Publishing Company flourished chiefly because of his tremendous sales. I don't mean that I can't keep going without him but I'll have to be a lot more cautious about the titles I publish from now on. There will be no big assured profits to help carry unknown writers until they get established."

"But Paula wasn't dependent on him," I pointed out. "She went on working, carrying her own weight."

"After all, Paula was — Paula."

I counted ten slowly. "How did she die, Mr. Webb? I want to know all the details."

His voice was colorless. "We don't know much. She was found in the swimming pool a couple of hours after Barry was discovered. She had killed herself. They were so terribly in love, you know."

"What makes you assume she killed herself?"

"Well, what else? Aside from the shock of Barry's death she had been acting rather queerly the last few days. The murder must have sent her right over the edge."

"But she could swim. I thought it was difficult for a swimmer to drown in a pool even if he wanted to. Instinctively —"

"It seems that she struck her head on a metal handgrip as she went in; there was evidence of that. Probably she was unconscious

42

when she entered the water."

"And how did Barry die?"

"Look here, are you sure you want to go into all this? It's pretty grim."

"I have to. For my own peace of mind."

He considered and then nodded. "Yes, I think that's the way I would feel too. Of course, the papers and radio and television have carried the whole thing. I don't know what I could add. Barry finished his book on Eliot Masters, you know, and he called me in New York to tell me he'd send it in by Paula the next day.

"Naturally I was excited. We were sure of book club rights, practically sure of a *Reader's Digest* selection, and the paperbacks had gone up in their bidding to a guarantee of $150,000. Barry sounded jubilant. It had been a long job and he always worked like a dog on his books, eight to nine hours a day, seven days a week, until he finished. For a creative writer those are killing hours. He told me to supply the champagne so we could celebrate when I came out for the weekend. That's the last time I ever heard him speak.

"You must have seen all the rest of it in the papers. Paula did not come in the next day. Late that afternoon Barry was found in his study. His skull had been cracked open. There was a piece of lead pipe on the floor beside him and evidence that it was the

43

weapon which had killed him. It came from the terrace where some repairs were being made on the swimming pool. And, of course, the big point was that the Masters script had disappeared."

"But how could anyone get in the house unnoticed?"

Dexter gave an exasperated sigh. "An army could get in that house unnoticed. I don't suppose anyone but Blanche ever thinks of locking a door. It's haphazard all the way except for Barry's study and his working hours. They were never broken in on."

"So Barry was really killed to prevent the book from being published."

Dexter turned for a swift, surprised look at me. "Well, of course. There is no other conceivable motive. Everyone else lost by his death. I hope to God I can find the carbon copies and get that book into print."

"You mean you haven't been able to find them?"

"Up to now, there's been no chance to look. The police took the keys to his files and sealed off the study. I understand I'll be able to get in tomorrow."

"What I can't figure out, Mr. Webb, is why the people behind the murder waited until the book was finished before taking action."

"I don't suppose we'll ever know the answer to that. Certainly if Barry had any requests to cease and desist, or any threats of

44

reprisals, he never mentioned them to me."

"As I recall, he usually publicized any kind of threat."

Again Dexter Webb turned swiftly toward me and then his eyes went back to the road. "You didn't like him much, did you?"

"I never even met him. But I didn't like his books. Oh, I realize they were brilliant, but it seemed to me that he pulled people down either because he was just plain sadistic or because he was jealous of anyone bigger than he was."

"Of course," Dexter said, "a lot of people felt that way. But you must remember there was no one bigger than he was in his own field. He was tops. His writing sparkled. It just — flowed." He was silent for a moment and I looked at his profile. A very nice profile.

"I'm not trying to deny that Barry made enemies," he said at length. "You can't help it unless you conform absolutely. But he made friends, too. Admirers. Devotees." He paused again. "Like Paula. One thing I'm sure of, Miss Wales, you never heard Paula criticize his work or his integrity, and she was in a better position than anyone else to evaluate him, both personally and professionally."

"I know. She thought he was wonderful."

The car had slowed down. Dexter said, "Oh, God! Well, here we are. Keep your chin up."

I hadn't been prepared for the line of cars drawn up at the side of that narrow country lane, for the men who piled out of them, equipped with cameras and microphones, for the flashlight pictures, for the barrage of questions. Dexter, shouting "No comment," put an arm around my shoulders, shielded me the best he could, and forced his way through the inquisitive crowd with the belated help of a policeman.

"Scavengers," he said, white-lipped. "Are you all right?"

"Yes. I didn't know people could be like that."

He smiled suddenly and it was a nice smile. "Not all of them are. These are just the things that come out from under stones." He added in an attempt to be fair, "And for some of them, of course, it's just a job."

The house, a big three-story building of cedar shingles and maroon shutters, was set well back from the road from which it was protected by a twelve-foot evergreen hedge. Inside, the place was broken up into a number of small rooms, all rather cluttered, rather shabby, and, as I was to learn later by daylight, rather dark. There was no trace here of Paula who loved light and air and color, who felt stifled by dark rooms.

At least a quarter of the ground floor space seemed to be wasted in large and drafty hallways, unexpected corridors, and closets bigger than the rooms they served. The only really comfortable rooms in the house — I learned this later, too — were Barry's study and his bedroom, both of which were luxurious, spacious, and sunlit.

That first evening all I really noticed were the people themselves. The woman who opened the door cautiously before admitting us was in her late thirties. She wore no make-up on her rather plain face and she was dressed in ill-fitting black. She looked from Dexter to me and then, rather pointedly, at my white dress.

"Ruth," Dexter said, "this is Paula's young sister, Sue Wales."

After the briefest of hesitations Ruth offered me a hand that was icy cold. "Yes, Warren told us you had arrived. Won't you come in?"

There were five people in the room and, as I stood in the doorway, facing that battery of hostile eyes, it felt like a firing squad. I was an intruder here. For a moment I thought no one was going to move or even acknowledge my existence. Dexter must have thought so, too, because he touched my arm lightly as though to remind me that he was standing by.

A stout woman in her late sixties, wearing deep mourning, came forward. "I am Barry's mother. So you are Paula's sister! My, how different you are." Her eyes, too, rested re-

47

proachfully on the white dress. "I believe Paula said you are an actress."

I muttered something, I don't know what. Then Mrs. Hamilton said, "You must meet my husband. He was very fond of Paula." She spoke as though this were some unaccountable eccentricity.

John Hamilton was tall and thin, and he looked like a poet, or the way a lyric poet is supposed to look; Shelley grown old, if one can imagine that. He had a gentle voice and a gentle manner. To my surprise he bent over and kissed my cheek lightly. "Welcome, my dear."

"Do sit down, Father," Ruth said fussily and almost pushed him into a chair. I noticed then that there was a tremor in his hands, but I had been wrong about the eyes. There, at least, I found no hostility.

"My daughter-in-law," Mrs. Hamilton said dryly. "Blanche, this is Paula's sister."

She was crowding fifty and not fighting it. She wasn't fighting weight either. She had a square face with small shrewd eyes, no trace of having been good looking, and more self-assurance than any human being I had ever encountered. She summed me up quickly and held out a hand that was plastered with diamonds.

"Where is your friend?" she asked in a voice like the rough side of a saw. "The Maitland man. Warren mentioned him. You've met Warren, of course. Our tame lawyer."

Warren King, who had got up as we came into the room, nodded without speaking.

The boyish type, Dexter had said. He was all that. At thirty-four he was trying to be a coltish twenty-two. He had a round face and a merry, youthful manner. He shook hands and gave me what was, I suppose, his mechanical response to all women, a look saying, "I'm willing if you are; how about it?" When I ignored this approach he lost interest. His wife, who had watched this mute exchange, smiled faintly. It occurred to me, with a kind of shock, that she knew exactly what she had bought and that she was satisfied with her bargain, but if she ever stopped being satisfied, Tommy would get short shrift. I think he knew that too.

"So you are the heiress!" Tommy said in his engagingly youthful way. I noticed then how cold his eyes were. He smiled. "How very brave of you to come here."

4

All in all, the brief visit to the Hamiltons was a little stinker. With the exception of Dexter Webb and John Hamilton they resented me bitterly. The worst of it was that I couldn't blame them. About the money, at least. But there was nothing to be done about that until I found out why Paula had changed her will.

What I did blame them for, what made me resent them as bitterly as they resented me, was their attitude in regard to my sister. So far as the Hamiltons were concerned her death — her suicide, as they kept repeating — appeared to be just a minor but embarrassing inconvenience, the act of an unbalanced woman, like her second will. What really counted was the loss of the great Barry, wonderful son, wonderful brother, wonderful husband, wonderful writer, and, though they didn't mention it, wonderful provider.

"This," John Hamilton said wearily, "is a house of mourning. I wish you could have visited us when it was a happy place."

"I had a job."

"An actress." Ruth made this sound like

50

strip tease. "I know myself what it means to have a job. I work part-time at a little gift shop. It isn't much, perhaps, but Barry had so many responsibilities and every little bit helps." She made that sound like taking in laundry.

"Ruth," Warren King said, "attempts too much. Always helping people."

"Well, I do what I can." Ruth smiled bravely.

"Paula worked too," I pointed out hotly. "Full time. And she didn't make a production of it." I looked at Tommy. "What's your job? I don't think Paula ever mentioned it."

At least no one can say I failed to justify all the original dislike the Hamiltons had for me. The only exception was Blanche who didn't care in the least. Probably she had no objection to an occasional reminder that Tommy was her property. The corners of Dexter's lips twitched and he struggled to hold back a laugh. Then his amusement faded as a gluey voice, which I recognized immediately, said, "Oh! I didn't know you had company. I just came down for my knitting."

"This is Paula's sister, Sue Wales. Luella Matthews, an old friend of the family."

Luella was a few years older than I, probably twenty-seven or a little more, fair-haired and with rather pretty features marred by eczema. She looked at me with the poorest

51

imitation of surprise I'd ever seen. Compared with her acting, I'm star material.

"Well," said the gluey voice, "this is a surprise. I didn't mean to interrupt. I'm so sorry."

"Come in, dear," Mrs. Hamilton called warmly. "You know you never interrupt anything." As Luella dropped onto a footstool beside Mrs. Hamilton's chair, the older woman smiled at me. "Luella is quite one of the family. In fact, at one time we thought — we hoped — she would be one of the family." She sighed. "But I've always made a practice of not interfering with my children's plans. After all, it's up to them to decide, isn't it? To make their own mistakes."

Enough is enough. I told them I'd had a long hot drive and I must get back to the inn. No one urged me to stay any longer.

"I'll take you back," Dexter said.

"Oh, Dex," Luella wailed, "there's something I've simply got to ask you about Barry's papers if you're to start working on them tomorrow."

"We can discuss it then. Plenty of time."

"I'll run Miss Wales back to the inn," the lawyer said rather grudgingly. "I have to pass it on my way home, anyhow."

Somewhat to my disappointment, this is the way it was settled. The Hamiltons said good night and hoped I'd get through the cordon of watchers in front. I'd be lucky if they didn't take my picture and involve me in all the ugly publicity. Especially if they learned my sister had been the suicide.

"But publicity is good for entertainers, isn't it?" Luella asked with an innocent air.

"One thing sure," Tommy said, "if the photographers don't get a picture of you, Mrs. Oliphant will."

For the first time I felt it, the almost unbearable tension in the air.

"Mrs. Oliphant?"

"Our next-door neighbor," Mrs. Hamilton explained. "She makes a hobby of candid camera shots and sometimes she is quite unscrupulous. She doesn't respect privacy and she isn't, I'm afraid, a very truthful woman."

I remembered then. "Oh, she took the pictures of Paula and Barry that appeared in the *New York Times*. I noticed the credit line."

"I do hope you get away all right." Ruth hustled me out of the room before I even had an opportunity to say good night.

Apparently the patient watchers had given up their vigil; at any rate, there was no one in sight. We were not molested as we started off. I don't remember either of us speaking on the way to the inn. As the lawyer helped me out of the car he said, "You'll let me know what your plans are."

"I don't know myself. Joe is handling everything for me."

"Oh, yes. Well, good night, Miss Wales."

"Thank you for the lift."

"I had to pass the inn, anyhow." The implication was clear that he wouldn't have brought me if it had taken him a foot out of his way.

Joe wasn't waiting in the lobby, which was another disappointment. I was bursting to pour all my fury at the Hamiltons into his long-suffering ears. Then I realized that he too had assumed that Dexter Webb would drive me back. Unlike me, Joe was nothing if not tactful.

I lay awake for a long time trying to imagine what Paula's married life had been like in the house where no one, with the possible exception of her father-in-law, had wanted her; no one, that is, except Dexter Webb who had loved her, who would have cherished her. But Paula, with that curious drive toward self-destruction, had chosen Barry instead.

One by one, I considered the Hamilton family. John Hamilton was an ineffectual dreamer, but he alone had been fond of Paula. Mrs. Hamilton had resented her for deposing her own choice, Luella the doormat, who would have made an ideal daughter-in-law because she was so amenable. I went on to Tommy and his wife Blanche, stout, ugly, an elderly forty-six, with a much younger husband and such magnificent self-assurance. One thing puzzled me about Blanche Hamilton. Why on earth did she consent to live with her husband's family who disliked her when she could afford to live elsewhere?

I found myself coming back to Tommy, coming back to the things he had said: *So you are the heiress! How very brave of you to come here.* Tommy was no intellectual heavyweight but he wasn't mentally retarded either. And his seemingly pointless reference to Mrs. Oliphant had been like a time bomb. You could hear the ticking, hear the Hamiltons waiting for the thing to go off.

I thumped my pillow and turned it over. My imagination was running away with me. But it continued to run, so I tried counting. Then I tried reciting verse. And I heard Dexter Webb say in that shaken voice: "Cover her face; mine eyes dazzle; she died young." I buried my face in the pillow.

II

Somewhere there was a sound like rain, which became the rustling of leaves. A thrush was singing its heart out, a song so lovely that I lay smiling, last night's tears forgotten. At last I opened my eyes reluctantly and observed for the first time how charming my room was with its fireplace and chintz-covered chairs, sunlight pouring in from a sweet-scented garden.

55

It was after nine and I got quickly out of bed. Country inns don't as a rule serve breakfast all morning and I was hungry. Joe was probably hungry too and waiting impatiently for me to appear.

While I dressed I wondered where I would spend the next night. The clerk had made clear that there were no rooms in Stockford and the Hamiltons were fresh out of hospitality. In any case, I didn't want to stay in a house where Paula had been so manifestly an interloper.

The telephone rang and, assuming it would be Joe at the end of his patience, I said quickly, "I'll be right down."

"Miss Wales?"

"Yes."

"I am Sarah Oliphant. Mrs. Oliphant. A neighbor of the Hamiltons."

"Oh, yes, they mentioned you last night."

"I'm not surprised." She sounded amused. "The local radio announced your arrival this morning. It occurred to me that you must be finding it difficult to get accommodations in Stockford as the place is simply bursting at the seams with tourists. So I wondered whether you'd like me to put you up for a time. I have a big house, plenty of room, and I enjoy having guests."

I was so taken aback I couldn't think of what to say. "That's terribly kind of you. I don't really have any plans yet. That is, a

56

friend of mine drove me over from Pennsylvania —"

"Joseph Wentworth Maitland. The radio announcer practically stuttered over his name. Well of course, you can bring him too. I have four empty guest rooms." Her voice was pleasant, warmly cordial. Then a laugh came over the wire, a big hearty uninhibited laugh. "Or perhaps the Hamiltons have scared you off. We seem to have a mutual non-admiration society. Except for Paula." She added simply, "I loved Paula."

"Thank you for telling me. May I call you as soon as I've talked to Joe? He's really — in a way — in charge of this expedition."

"By all means. Just let me know what you decide."

Joe was waiting in the lobby. Instead of looking irritable, as I assumed to be the custom of unfed males, he was unusually cheerful. One reason for this, I discovered as he led the way to the coffee shop where breakfast was served, was that he had been sensible enough to have breakfasted an hour earlier.

"And what have you been up to?" I asked suspiciously.

"Coffee first, news later."

When I had disposed of cantaloupe, cereal, bacon, eggs, and toast, he shook his head. "How do you do it? Another year and you'll weigh two hundred pounds."

"I haven't gained an ounce in fifteen months, and I don't know what you find so funny."

"You — waging a losing battle between a desire to exchange news and a desire to replenish the inner man."

As I said, you simply can't feel romantic about Joe. I smoldered for a moment but gave up. You can't fight with him either, because he won't fight back. I had never seen him really lose his temper. At least, not up to that time.

So I told him about my evening with the Hamiltons, trying not to dramatize, to report accurately, and ended with the unexpected telephone call a few minutes earlier from Mrs. Oliphant.

"The Hamiltons' next-door neighbor? That's wonderful, Sue. I hope you accepted for both of us."

"I said I'd have to consult you."

Joe's round eyes studied me quizzically. "Why this unaccustomed but flattering deference to my opinion?"

"I gathered from the Hamiltons that the woman is a busybody."

"Fine! What more could you ask? What are we waiting for?"

"And the Hamiltons dislike her. They" — I tried to describe the strained atmosphere after Tommy had mentioned Mrs. Oliphant, and how Ruth had practically pushed me

58

out of the house.

"For my money, that settles it. Call her back and say we'll be around this morning, if that's convenient for her."

"This is going to cause trouble with the Hamiltons," I warned him.

"What are you afraid of, Sue? There's no love lost between you now, is there?"

"I wish to God we hadn't come here!" I burst out. "Something is wrong. Everyone tells me Paula was out of her mind. She wasn't. She wasn't. I'm going to prove she wasn't."

"Your voice carries," Joe said quietly. "That's one thing the theater has taught you. Now go get your stuff together and call Mrs. Oliphant while I take care of the bill."

As I went into the lobby I saw Ruth Hamilton moving away from the coffee shop and wondered if she had overheard my outburst. She crossed the lobby and unlocked the door of one of those tourist-bait places that sells postcards printed in New Jersey, cigarette cases made in New Mexico, and other "New England" souvenirs direct from Japan.

Mrs. Oliphant said she was delighted to know that she could put us up and our rooms were waiting for us. She looked forward to our arrival.

After all, Joe didn't seem to be in such an all-fired hurry to get to her house. He listened with only half his attention to my account of Ruth Hamilton's scuttling away from the coffee shop as I came out.

"Perhaps she was eavesdropping. The Hamiltons are going to watch every step you take, Sue. Might as well accept the idea now. If they can find any way of breaking Paula's will —"

"Unsound mind," I reminded him bitterly.

"But she was perfectly normal when she talked to you shortly before her death."

"Yes, but that was a telephone call and it's not evidence. Anyhow, if I wanted the money I'd be sure to say that, wouldn't I? Even Dexter Webb says something was wrong with her, and he loved her, Joe. You can't mistake that."

"I thought so, too," he said gently. "Look here, do you mind if we drive around a bit before we tackle the Oliphant woman? I want to talk and I don't know what kind of setup we'll encounter there, how much privacy we are going to have."

In a few minutes he had found a country lane that wound up and down hill, around dairy farms and past an abandoned mill and a cemetery whose slanting stones bore faded names that had been carved long before the Revolution.

He pulled up beside a stone wall, shut off the motor, and lighted his pipe while I followed the flight of a cardinal, a crimson flash across the blue sky.

"While you were with the Hamiltons last night I made some long distance calls. Took me quite a while. I wanted to talk to Eliot Masters direct. God! Why does anyone want the big jobs? I went through channels I'd never heard of. But naturally I kept at it."

I grinned, wondering what kind of opposition it would take to stop Joe once he had made up his mind to do something.

"Not only is the big boy protected by the little boys, but the Governor is also ducking the press and all the people with questions about the missing script. I finally got through to him."

"How did you manage it?"

"Well," Joe sounded embarrassed, "I've put a bit into the campaign fund. I didn't like using that as a lever but there was no other choice."

"What did you expect he would do? Confess?"

"Confess! Don't be more of an idiot than you can help, woman. I wanted to urge him to hold off his decision about running in the primaries. I said I couldn't guarantee anything but I had a hunch we might be able to track down Barry Hamilton's killer and take the heat off him. Masters," he said flatly, "seemed to like the idea."

"Of all the understatements! I'll bet he did. But if Dexter Webb goes ahead with the book — that's supposing he can find carbon copies

61

— I don't see how you can help Masters."

"Look here, Sue, we've all been hypnotized by the headlines and the ballyhoo; we assumed they knew what they were talking about. But when I gave it a moment's quiet thought I realized no one from the Masters faction would steal that book and leave a dead body to mark the spot."

"But the fact remains that Barry was slugged and that someone stole his book on Masters."

"True, O queen."

"And only someone interested in the Masters campaign, whether for or against, would want the script."

"Now that's where you are way off the beam. I'll admit," Joe said magnanimously, "I was taken in at first, too. The murder of Barry and the missing script — take them together and you get Eliot Masters. But suppose you don't take them together? Before Barry Hamilton ever thought of the Masters book he was well toward the top of the list as one of America's best-hated men. There's a wide field to cover."

"But if he was killed for some other reason, why steal the Masters script?"

"A red herring. A perfectly dazzling and completely confusing red herring. Hamilton is murdered; his book on Masters disappears. *Ergo,* Masters masterminded the murder. Why look elsewhere? So far as I can make out, no one has looked elsewhere."

I was silent — for me — a long time. "But we both believe that Paula looked elsewhere; anyhow, that she knew or suspected who killed Barry."

"If you can dream up any other reason for killing her I'll play along."

"And what happens if the murderer believes she told me? Joe, I want to go home."

"That's no way to handle it."

"You'd turn me loose on a murderer," I began furiously.

"I'll be here, and not just because you've become a habit with me either. There are two strings to my bow, Sue: you and Masters. I want him in the clear."

"And I suppose my dead body will be laid at the foot of his shrine as a fitting sacrifice."

"There are times when that doesn't appear to be a bad idea." Joe started the car. "Watch it, Sue," he said soberly. "You have a low boiling point and you reach it the moment anyone looks cross-eyed at Paula; but we've got a job to do. Try not to lose your temper. Find out what other people think before you express your own opinion. And don't volunteer one single damned thing."

"What do you think we can find out? Honestly, Joe, what can we do that the police can't do better, and how are we going to do it?"

"I don't know how, but I know what. Last night I drew up a list of questions as a

63

starter." He handed it to me.

a) Who murdered Barry and why?
b) Who murdered Paula and why?
c) What did Paula want you to do?
d) Why did she change her will before Barry's death?
e) What message did she leave you and where is it?
f) Why was the script stolen and where is it now?
g) Who, except for Barry himself, knew what was in it?
h) Why all the stink about Paula's second will?

"That looks very businesslike," I said. One thing I was learning: if, day in and day out, I was going to have to talk about Paula's death I had better tackle it as impersonally as possible or I'd break down altogether. I fought savagely to thrust away the pictures that kept crowding into my mind of someone pushing her into the pool, slamming her head against the handgrip, holding her head under until she drowned. Paula, so lovely and so sweet.

"At least," I said, "we don't have to ask how or when or where they were killed. About the missing script — that must have been destroyed, of course."

"But what about carbon copies, notes, material? It stands to reason that an outsider

64

might have picked up the finished script. But would he — or she — know where to look for the man's notes and all that?"

"Dexter Webb will probably find out today whether there are any copies of the script. The police are going to unseal the study and turn over the keys to him."

"By the way, did Barry type his own stuff?"

"I have no idea how he worked." After a moment I said, "Joe, about Paula's will . . ."

"I know of a good man in New York. The family has used him for years in checking on financial positions of people they doubted. I'm going to put him to work checking on the finances of these people. It would be interesting to find out if one of them needs money in a hurry. That could explain a lot, you know."

"Apparently they all need money. Except Tommy, of course. Though how he could have married that awful woman, even to be supported . . . !"

"Well, there's a long way to go yet."

"So far," I reminded him, "we haven't gone anywhere."

"We're starting now. First stop, Mrs. Oliphant."

5

As we drove past the evergreen hedge that shut off the Hamilton house from the road, I pointed it out to Joe. This morning there was only one car pulled up on the side, but whether the bored man at the wheel was a reporter or a detective I couldn't tell.

Joe flicked a hand at him and the man waved. "What a place to stake out! A country lane with no place to hide, nowhere to take cover."

"A policeman's lot is not a happy one."

"That wasn't the police."

"How do you know?"

"Ran into him this morning. A nice fellow. New York paper. He was looking for you, as a matter of fact."

"He didn't bother me."

"He won't bother you. We — uh — talked it over."

Unlike the Hamiltons, Mrs. Oliphant did not seek seclusion. A beautifully kept lawn ran down to the road, set off only by a trim border of flowers. The driveway curved to the front door of a rambling frame structure with late nineteenth century turrets and stained-glass windows, and an open porch with a balcony above. Wherever a pillar could be placed, a pillar was used.

Joe slid out from under the wheel and came around to help me out of the car. In answer to his ring a pleasant-looking woman in a neat uniform came to the door.

"I am Miss Wales. Mrs. Oliphant is expecting us."

The house was built on a simple old-fashioned plan. A wide hallway bisected it, rooms on either side, with an unexpectedly handsome carved mahogany staircase. The housekeeper led us up the stairs to a big sunny bedroom.

Mrs. Oliphant was a lighthearted sixty, her white hair innocent of a rinse but carefully set, her face unexpectedly tanned. She had really lovely blue eyes, discreet makeup on a full mouth, and a face that, though it would never have been called pretty, must always have been interesting. She was, I thought, exceptionally small. I say, "I thought," because it wasn't easy to tell. She sat in a deep chair, a footstool in front of it, and on the footstool was resting a leg in a plaster cast.

She held out both hands. "Come here, my dear. As you see, I can't get up to welcome you." She took my hands in a warm grasp, looking up with those lovely eyes, which were both interested and kind.

I fell for her at once and, while she still

held my hands, eased myself gingerly onto the footstool so I wouldn't jar the cast.

"You've been so kind, Mrs. Oliphant," I began.

She smiled, a smile as mischievous as a girl's. "Never trust people who appear kind. I asked you because I wanted you, partly because you are Paula's sister, and partly —"

"Because you are simply dying of curiosity," Joe told her.

Her eyes moved over him, her beautifully groomed brows rose. "And who is that obnoxious young man, my dear?"

"He is Joe Maitland and he has the manners of a stablehand."

Her eyes twinkled at him. "At least, he is neither a fool nor a hypocrite, and that should make a refreshing change."

"And how," he asked, "do you categorize your neighbors next door?"

"I'm not sure which category they go in. It's easy to strip the mask from a hypocrite, but not so easy from someone who wants to appear a fool." She turned from Joe to me. "You are both to feel perfectly free to come and go as you please. I'd love having you for meals but you are to do as you like about that too. Just let Carry know in advance. Simply because I'm tied by the leg doesn't mean that I need looking after. I absolutely refused to go to the hospital. For some reason, doctors aren't satisfied with looking after you any more. They take to tests the way an addict does to drugs. Dr. Ames, knowing me, didn't waste time arguing."

"How did it happen?" I asked idly.

"I still haven't worked that out."

Joe, who had been looking at the original Matisse on the wall, stiffened like a pointer. "This must be an awkward time to have guests, extra work for your staff and all that." He was watching her closely.

She returned his look. "Couldn't be a better time, Mr. Maitland. I'm putting you in the room behind this one, just in case I should need a bodyguard. It's nice to have a man in the house. Sometimes I think the most tiresome thing about growing old is that a woman is eventually forced into the company of other women." She smiled at him. "And you, Miss Wales . . ."

"Won't you call me Sue?"

"Sue, I'll put you across the hall from me. In Paula's room."

"Paula's!"

"Why, yes. She moved over here the day before Barry was murdered."

For once I was speechless. I simply gaped at her.

"Mrs. Oliphant," Joe declared, "you are the star on the Christmas tree. You are the answer to a prayer. May I kiss you?" Without waiting for her reply he bent over to kiss her cheek.

69

The lovely eyes twinkled at him. "It had occurred to me," she said demurely, "that the Hamiltons might not mention it."

"Was there," I demanded, "anything wrong with Paula's mind?"

"Except for her misguided taste in husbands, nothing at all," Mrs. Oliphant replied with emphasis.

"Were the police told that she left her husband the day before his death and that she was staying with you?"

"You will have to ask them about that. The day Barry was murdered, when all the excitement was at its height, I broke my leg. I was *hors de combat.* In any case, the police wouldn't have questioned me. Why should they?"

"And you don't know how it happened?" Joe asked in an odd voice.

"Of course I know how; I just don't know why. I was pushed down the stairs."

"Pushed!" After a moment Joe said, "You mean it was deliberate? Someone tried to kill you?"

"The strange thing was, you know, that I had put on a heavy beach robe of Paula's because I was chilly. Quite an unmistakable robe, wide green and yellow stripes."

Mrs. Oliphant looked at us, her eyes very bright.

11

"So that is why you wanted Sue to come," Joe said at last.

Mrs. Oliphant's hands tightened on the arms of her chair. "I loved Paula and I think she was fond of me. When she asked whether I could put her up for a day or so, I didn't bother her with questions. Clearly something had gone very wrong with that marriage. I didn't have the feeling that this was some lovers' quarrel that could be patched up.

"Then I was thrown down the stairs and broke my leg. Paula came running and sent for the doctor. He had just come from the Hamilton house and he had to break the news of Barry's murder to her. And she saw that I was wearing her robe and I think she knew the accident had been meant for her. It must have been hell. But she stayed there, helping the doctor with the cast. So white and still! And only when I was all right did she go over to the other house. But one thing I am sure of, when she died in that pool it wasn't while of unsound mind."

She swallowed and took a long breath. "And that is the last emotional storm you'll have to put up with from me, but it had to be said." She looked at a small gold clock on the mantel. "I know you'll want to unpack and get settled. Lunch at one fifteen, sherry at one. Perhaps you'll have your sherry with me."

71

Her smile dismissed us. We found the housekeeper hovering in the hall, waiting to show us our rooms, which, as our hostess had said, were ready, including, in mine at least, a bowl of fragrant roses.

Joe was waiting downstairs when I had finished unpacking. I ran to him, clinging to him for the first time in my life, my face pressed against his shoulder. He stood patting me awkwardly as though I were a nervous horse.

"Joe, there's no doubt about it now, is there? Paula was murdered."

"No doubt at all. And I was wrong to bring you here. I'm sending you back as of today and I'll stay on alone. I don't think Mrs. Oliphant will mind. I like her, don't you?"

"I'm not going back, Joe. I'm not scared any more. Just blazingly angry. I'm going to stay until we find out who did that to Paula."

Joe wasn't happy about it. "Well, if you are sure . . ."

"I never was so sure of anything in my life."

Carry, the housekeeper, came down the hall and looked at us in surprise. Joe said, "Let's go out for a while." Being Joe he headed for a couple of lawn chairs under a big umbrella. "You know, I thought there was a chance we might pick up something here but I never dreamed of this. We've learned a

72

terrific amount so far. First, Paula and Barry had come to a parting of the ways. Second, an attempt was made to kill her shortly after Barry's murder, and the killer got Mrs. Oliphant instead. Only — hey, do you think it would be possible to make that mistake?"

I nodded. I had already thought of it. "She is tiny, Joe. I imagine she is just about Paula's size. And her white hair — you remember how fair Paula was. If a person expected Paula . . ."

"Yes." Joe took his time before he went on. "One thing," he said quietly, "this washes out not only Masters but the whole damned political angle."

"Why?"

"Think it out for yourself."

I thought. "Oh, of course, a stranger would not have recognized Paula's beach robe." I found myself shivering though the temperature was already eighty. "Somehow, that makes it worse, doesn't it? It means that it has to be someone next door."

"Obviously that is what Mrs. Oliphant believes. You've seen them all, Sue. Who is your candidate?"

"Tommy," I said promptly.

"And what was his motive? Of the lot, he is the best off financially, so far as we know. At least his wife is."

"I don't know. But I do know now why Paula changed her will. Because she had left

73

Barry. She never expected me to inherit his estate."

"Would she have done that at once?"

"When she made up her mind she never hesitated."

"So what do we have? Paula had left Barry. He was murdered. In mistake for Paula, Mrs. Oliphant was injured just a short time later. Paula went to the Hamilton house, tried to telephone you, and was drowned. And somewhere, somehow, she tried to get a message to you."

"Well, what are we going to do about it? I can't see what you are looking so cheerful about, except that your hero is in the clear."

"Sure, I'm glad about that," Joe agreed, "though there isn't an ounce of proof, one way or another. Nothing for the police. Nothing to gladden the heart of Eliot Masters. What pleases me is that there is no further need to hunt for a needle in a haystack, an anonymous hireling who might be a party hack. We've narrowed the field to — how many people: Mr. Hamilton, Mrs. Hamilton, Ruth, Tommy, Blanche, and Luella Matthews. Six suspects."

"The only drawback is that every single one of them stood to lose by Barry's death. The only thing I am sure of is that Paula was as sane as you are."

After a long pause Joe said, "Perhaps you

74

would be smart not to say that around here."

"Why?"

"I don't know why. Call it a hunch."

A couple of hours later I got the answer.

6

At twelve thirty Carry came to tell us that Mrs. Oliphant's physician, Dr. Ames, was there. As he had also attended the Hamiltons we might like to talk to him. If so, we would find him in her room.

When we got there the doctor had finished his examination. He was slightly under middle height, with a long oval face that looked as though he never had enough rest, observant eyes, and a forthright manner. We got a taste of that as we went in.

". . . your own fault, you know. If you will go wandering around the place, not looking where you are going, what do you expect? Next time, you'll probably break a hip."

"Next time," she retorted, "bring your bedside manner with you, Dick."

"This is my bedside manner," he snapped, and they both laughed. I gathered they were old friends as well as doctor and patient.

"It was broad daylight," she said. "I've told you that over and over. Five o'clock in the afternoon. I'd finished my bath and started to dress for dinner when I heard someone in the hall. I grabbed a robe and went out."

"I still don't see how you fell down that flight of stairs."

Mrs. Oliphant caught sight of us. "Come in, Sue. I want you to know Dr. Ames. Dick, this is Paula Hamilton's young sister, Miss Wales. And Mr. Maitland."

"You have my deepest sympathy for your loss, Miss Wales. Your sister was a lovely person. So young to die. So needless. She would have recovered from the shock of her husband's death in time. People do, you know. They must, if the world is to go on."

"You were her physician, weren't you?" Joe asked when the two men had shaken hands.

"Hardly. She was in fine health. The only consultation we ever had was about her husband. She thought he was working too hard. He was, of course, but that's the way he wanted it."

"Was Hamilton in bad health?" Joe asked in surprise.

"By the time he finished a book his blood pressure was always too high, but then he would knock off for a few months and get back to normal."

"What about Paula's mental condition?" I asked as steadily as I could. That one point I intended to clear up if I died for it, and I nearly did.

"I'd have said she was a completely normal, healthy human being, and that is rarer than you may think. But, of course,

77

when she killed herself she was stunned by her husband's death. I was the one who had to tell her about it. At the time she seemed to be taking it all right. Terribly quiet, of course, but I thought that was simply control she was exercising for Mrs. Oliphant's sake, because Mrs. Oliphant had just broken her leg and was in great pain. No one can foresee how people will react to shock."

He expressed his sympathy again, told Mrs. Oliphant not to go playing Lady Macbeth if she didn't want to break her neck, and went quickly down the stairs. A man who never had time to catch up with the demands on him.

Carry brought in a tray with a decanter of sherry, glasses, and some biscuits. For a few moments Mrs. Oliphant's conversation was rather vague, her attention divided between us and a blue bird on the branch of a Japanese maple on the lawn. She held her camera, snapped it, and put it down with a look of satisfaction.

"That should really be a beauty in color, the contrast between the vivid blue of the bird and the red of the maple."

"Hobby of yours?" Joe asked.

She laughed. "I never can be just halfway interested in things. I go whole hog. And now, laid up like this, it is great fun. I had no idea so much went on in a garden." She smiled up mischievously at Joe who had fallen for her as hard as I had.

He was standing beside her chair, looking out past the garden toward the Hamilton house. From this second-story window there was a clear view over the hedge, which separated the two properties, and of the side of the house, the swimming pool at the back, and a small guesthouse on the rear of the property.

"Is that a separate entrance?" Joe asked.

"Yes, it leads to Barry's study. He could come and go as he liked without running into callers."

"Very convenient." Joe looked not at the door to Barry's study but at the binoculars on the table beside Mrs. Oliphant's chair, a table crowded with a princess phone, a small radio, and a tiny television set.

"Very," she agreed shamelessly. Then, as she saw the expression in his face her smile faded. "Oh, no, Joe! I didn't see the murderer. My God, I wouldn't keep still about a thing like that." As Carry came in with her lunch tray she said, "Your lunch is ready. Usually I rest for a while in the afternoon."

As soon as the meal was over I went outdoors, leaving Joe to his own devices. This time I went around the other side of the house, crossed the lawn, and walked along the hedge until I found an opening. I headed for the swimming pool where Paula had died. For a long time I stared down at the water

79

sparkling in the afternoon sun. The pool was larger than I had expected and deeper, a long oval, blue-tiled. At one end there was a stone terrace with the usual canopy and chairs and tables, and a door leading into the house. Crouching down, I looked at the metal handgrip where Paula had been knocked out, and I wondered who had knelt where I was kneeling now, who had held Paula's head under water.

Paula had been found in the pool in broad daylight, when the house was still filled with police. It didn't seem credible that anyone would take such a terrible risk of being caught red-handed. For the first time my assurance that Paula had not committed suicide was shaken.

Somewhere a telephone was ringing. Then I saw the small telephone on the wall of the house beyond the terrace. The ringing broke off as the telephone was answered on another extension inside. My eyes rested on that small phone. This must be where Paula had made that desperate call to me, the call so sharply broken off.

In the back of my mind I had been aware of the sound of typing. Now it stopped. I turned to see Luella Matthews standing in the door of Barry's study, watching me. I waved to her and started to call a greeting. Something in her manner stopped me cold.

She walked straight toward me. In the piti-

80

less daylight her complexion was worse than ever but, curiously enough, she was prettier today than she had been last night. There was more life in her, a kind of glow. Or perhaps it was just anger, for she was very angry and all her anger was directed at me.

"Last night," she began abruptly, her voice high and overwrought, "Tommy said you were brave to come here." As she had not been in the room at the time, I realized she must have been deliberately eavesdropping. "What I say is that you have a colossal nerve. Didn't she do enough harm without you coming here, stirring things up, bringing That Man with you?" I put that in caps because it's the way Luella made it sound.

"Joe?" I asked stupidly. "You mean Joe?"

"The Maitland man. What did you think he could do? Buy us off?"

If I hadn't been so staggered I'd have laughed at that, and then I was flamingly angry. "Look here, I'm not trying to buy anyone off. Neither is Joe. All we want is to know the truth. Who killed Paula?"

"Killed her? She killed herself. How many times do you need to be told?"

"Why?"

"Heartbreak, shock, mental instability. Take your choice. You name it, she had it. How should I know?" The words were vicious and yet they sounded childishly spiteful, almost flippant.

81

"I don't believe you. I've just been talking to Mrs. Oliphant. She said there was nothing wrong with Paula."

"You had better assume that there was, Miss Wales."

"Why?"

"You really are a witch, Luella." Tommy and Dexter had come from the guesthouse in bathing trunks, towels slung over their shoulders. "How you manage to pull the wool over the eyes of my poor misguided parents I can't imagine. A child could see through you. Your jealousy, your vindictive —"

"Take it easy, Tommy," Dexter said.

Tommy looked at him, shrugged, dropped his towel on the chair, and dived into the pool.

Dexter smiled at me. "Good afternoon. How's the cordon?"

"She didn't come that way," Luella told him. "She's staying at Mrs. Oliphant's. Snooping. Trying to make trouble. I warned her —"

"We heard you, Luella. And unless Mrs. Oliphant is deaf she probably heard you too." He put his hand on her shoulder. "You're terribly upset and you've been going over Barry's accounts ever since they opened the study. Take a break, get your bathing suit, and have some fun for a change."

"I thought you'd be working with me."

"I'll come later."

"Dex, did you find those ginger cookies I baked for you? I left them in the guest-house."

"I did indeed. Wonderful. Hop into that suit."

She gave him a wavering smile and then went into the house.

From the pool Tommy called, "I don't think much of your taste, Dex. Why bother with Luella when we have Miss Wales? Look here, Gypsy Girl, why don't you borrow a suit if you haven't one and join us?"

"Not today, thanks." I'd never go in that pool. "You go ahead," I told Dexter.

"There's no hurry." He pushed his hair out of his eyes impatiently. "Mrs. Oliphant must be having a field day."

"She's a darling," I said, "and, of course, it's convenient."

"Of course." There was laughter in his eyes. "Are you planning to turn detective, Sue?"

"I'll leave that to the experts. Dexter," we had arrived fast it seemed at first-name terms, but it was natural, "why was everyone so afraid to have Joe and me know Mrs. Oliphant?"

He groped for cigarettes on the table, offered me one, lighted them both. "You won't rest until you know, will you?"

"No."

"All right." He sounded tired, drained of

83

vitality. "But I wish to God you could leave it alone. For Paula's sake."

"That's just why I can't."

He glanced toward the pool, but Tommy was diving, paying no attention to us. "When I got up here that night they were both dead. The one thing that stood out like a beacon was that the Masters book had disappeared. I assumed as everyone did that they had been killed because of the book. Then the next day I learned that Paula and Barry had had a terrific quarrel and she had moved over to Mrs. Oliphant's the day before. And then Luella told us — well, there was nothing else to believe. That's why I went along with the Hamiltons about Paula being — unlike herself. It was the only out I could see for her. You'll have to take it, Sue. I'm terribly afraid Paula killed both Barry and herself."

7

"Look here," Dexter said in concern, "you had better sit down. I didn't mean to throw it at you that way but . . ." His hand guided me into a chair. "We ought to have a talk. I'll dress. Only take five minutes. Will you wait? We'll get out of here and take a drive."

I nodded and he ran across the lawn to the guesthouse. There was a moment when I couldn't think at all. Then I tried to pull my scattered thoughts together. Dexter had loved her and yet he believed Paula had committed murder.

"Hey!" The playful Tommy was bobbing up and down at my end of the pool. He splashed water within inches of my shoes. "Come on, Gypsy Girl. Get a suit and join me. The water's wonderful. Anyhow," and he gave me a boyish grin, "I want to see if you're that brown all over."

"That," Blanche said in her rasping voice, "is what I thought." She eased her square, heavy body into one of the metal chairs on the terrace and looked from Tommy to me. There was no particular hostility in her manner; she was quite simply prepared to sit it out and make sure her property wasn't being appropriated.

It was funny and it was grotesque. I wanted to assure her that I wouldn't have Tommy as a gift. The screen door onto the terrace slammed and Luella came out wearing a conservative suit and pulling a cap over her fair hair. Blanche gave her a quick look and turned back to me. Apparently she did not regard Luella as dangerous.

As though reading my thoughts she said, her words loud enough to reach Luella, "Whenever people talk about virtue being its own reward, I think of Luella. She knocks herself out to please. And she loses every time. First it was Barry and now it's Dexter, and both of them in love with Paula. She's one person, I can tell you, who shed no tears when your sister's body was discovered."

God knows she had fired point-blank but she seemed to have missed her target. Luella paused on the brink of the pool. "I guess you forget," she said in her gluey voice, "that all the responsibility fell on me. Dear Mrs. Hamilton collapsed, Ruth had hysterics, and you — sleeping pills, wasn't it? You didn't show up for hours, as I remember." She balanced for a moment and plunged into the pool.

Blanche's small eyes followed her with a look that made me shiver. Then she said casually, "How's the line out front?"

"I don't know. I came across the back lawn.

86

Mrs. Oliphant has kindly asked Joe and me to stay with her. Wasn't it nice? We might have had to go miles to find accommodations."

"You're staying with Sarah Oliphant?" The words seemed to be jolted out of her. "What does she want, a box seat for the Hamilton scandals?" She pushed back her chair with a grating sound — everything about Blanche Hamilton seemed to grate — and heaved herself up. "I've got things to do," she said abruptly and went into the house.

It was a relief when Dexter came across the lawn, wearing slacks and a sport shirt. Luella and Tommy were swimming sedately up and down the pool without exchanging a word.

"Sorry that we have to run the gantlet again. I ought to leave the car in the village."

We went around the house, past the door of Barry's study, and got into the Chrysler. This afternoon there were only three cars parked in the lane and, after a quick look, no one bothered us. The drivers sat slumped behind the wheels of their cars, one of them reading a newspaper, one a paperback, and one working a crossword puzzle.

"Who are they and what are they waiting for? What do they think is going to happen now? It's all over."

"I don't know whether they are reporters or detectives."

"Detectives?"

"Private, not police. I imagine both parties are keeping an eye on the place. There's a lot at stake for them. Any choice of direction?"

"Wherever you like." I leaned back, letting the soft wind blow my hair.

Dexter drove through the village, pointing out landmarks and then the Chrysler took a steep hill like a leaping cat. Five miles farther on, where the road leveled out, there was a wide observation point for people who wanted to enjoy the view. Dexter pulled in there and shut off the motor. I looked out and down on miles of fruit trees, cattle, streams sparkling in the sunlight, white farmhouses with red barns. It was all beautiful and peaceful.

Dexter was relaxed behind the wheel, apparently quite content with the silence broken only by an industrious woodpecker and the occasional swish of a car going by.

"Dexter, I can't imagine where you got the horrible idea that Paula was the murderer."

"Good God," he said softly, "you don't think I wanted to believe it! Not Paula."

"You loved her, didn't you?"

"Yes, I loved her. So did Barry. His love was the dominating thing in his life, more important than his work, bigger than his vanity." He saw my expression. "Naturally he was vain. He had tremendous talent, he was a success while still young, he was personally

88

attractive. Damn it, he had a right to be vain. But he put Paula first always and yet she — for some reason we'll never know — she quarreled with him the day before he died, moved over to Mrs. Oliphant's house. Didn't she tell you that?"

I shook my head. "She called me to tell me about Barry's murder. She was horribly upset. I think she must have been using that phone on the terrace. With the house filled with police she could hardly have made a private call from inside."

"But what did she say?"

"She didn't tell me that anything had happened between them. She wanted me to do something for her. She said I'd understand her message. She sounded — desperate."

"What message?"

"I don't know. She started to tell me where she had put it, and then she was interrupted and broke off."

"And you haven't found this message?"

I shook my head. "That's one reason I came here, that and to prove she didn't kill herself."

"Oh, my dear!" He sounded despairing.

"Dexter, you must have known as well as Mrs. Oliphant that there was nothing wrong with Paula's mind."

"Yes, I knew."

There was no point in polite evasions at this juncture. I asked bluntly, "Why did you

89

lie to me about that?"

"Because I wanted some kind of — excuse for her, if Luella talked, and she wasn't here to defend herself." He lifted one hand and dropped it on the wheel. "I made a mess of things, didn't I?" He looked profoundly unhappy.

"What could Luella have said?" When he made no reply I said, "Then I'll have to ask her."

"Luella," he said at last reluctantly, "was outside the study that afternoon. She heard them quarreling. Then she heard Barry say, 'Paula. Oh, don't!' And there was a thud. Luella waited for quite a while in her own room and then came back. She found Barry dead. Paula had gone."

He waited for me to speak and at last went on, "Well, later, she found Paula in the pool. Drowned. She believed she had killed herself in remorse. Meanwhile, of course, the loss of the Masters script was discovered. There was no time really to talk things over and decide what was best to do. After Barry married, Luella sort of turned to me for advice but, of course, it was hours before I got there that night.

"Next morning Warren told us about Paula's second will. It was a tremendous shock to the Hamiltons. Warren suggested the idea of suicide while of unsound mind, and we all agreed to go along with it; the

90

Hamiltons because they wanted to get Barry's estate and I because I didn't know any other way to protect Paula's name if Luella should talk. And Luella," he added, "isn't particularly reliable."

"Has it occurred to you," I asked, and I could hear the hostility in my voice though I was trying to keep calm, "that Luella may have killed Paula?"

With an impatient gesture, he thrust back his hair which fell over his forehead. "Oh, my dear! You are grasping at straws. If you can make yourself believe that Luella could kill anyone . . ."

"Easier than I could believe that Paula was capable of violence. I simply can't, Dexter."

"That's what I would have thought too. But that quarrel Luella overhead — there's no other possible explanation."

"Dexter," I said impulsively, because I couldn't hold it back any longer, "you don't need to have that nightmare of Paula as the murderer. She wasn't."

He half smiled. "How young you sound! How sure!"

"I am sure. Someone tried to kill Paula just a few minutes after Barry died, and nearly killed Mrs. Oliphant instead. That's how her leg was broken."

"What!"

In answer to his questions I told him about Mrs. Oliphant's having borrowed Paula's

91

beach robe and being thrown down the stairs. He listened intently, at first with hope lighting his face and then with it fading. What it all boiled down to, he said, was that Mrs. Oliphant was wearing Paula's robe. She hadn't seen anyone. She thought she was pushed. Older people hate to admit that their hearing or vision is fading, that they may be uncertain on their feet. The chances were if she had just got out of her bath that she hadn't been wearing her glasses. She thought she had been mistaken for Paula. Or — she said so.

"You don't believe her?"

His grin was rueful. "I wish to God I could. Has she told this to anyone else?"

"Well, to Joe, of course. But I'm sure she hasn't been broadcasting it. She's not at all the kind of person the Hamiltons believe. We talked to her physician before lunch and she hadn't told him, though he was needling her about bumbling around the place without looking where she was going." I swallowed. "She believed in Paula absolutely."

"God knows I don't want any shadow cast on Paula's memory but, if Mrs. Oliphant is to be believed, you have to make an incredible assumption: that the murderer, on the evidence of the beach robe, was someone at the Hamilton house."

"Well?" I challenged him defiantly.

"Well, my dear, who? Do we assume that

Barry was bashed over the head in cold blood by his own father or mother, by his sister or brother? For God's sake, Sue, this is Stockford, Connecticut. We aren't taking part in the Orestes trilogy."

"But there are also Blanche and Luella and Warren King, who aren't Hamiltons."

"Warren doesn't live at the house. He wasn't there."

"How do you know? You said yourself that anyone could get in."

"Get in the Hamilton house perhaps. But into Mrs. Oliphant's? Any reason why?"

"I don't know what reason Blanche might have, though I wouldn't put anything past her. But Luella hated Paula."

"And loved Barry," Dexter pointed out. "Are you predicating two murderers?"

"I gathered that Luella had sort of shifted her affections to you after he got married. At least, that is Blanche's idea."

There wasn't, of course, much that Dexter could say tactfully about that. "Do you really suspect Warren, whom Blanche calls our tame lawyer?"

"Is he? Tame, I mean."

Dexter shrugged. "He is just a village attorney and I imagine Barry was his biggest client. He handled his business affairs as well as his contracts and all that. Why on earth would he kill him? The goose that laid the golden eggs. Anyhow, Warren is the cautious

93

type, if I ever saw one. I don't think he would stick his chin out, whatever the provocation."

"If only Paula had had time to tell me! Of course, things must have been horribly upset at the house."

Dexter was silent, reliving the terrible hour after he arrived at the Hamilton house, hours later. "No," he said abruptly, "I simply can't accept the idea that anyone hated Paula enough to kill her. It's incredible."

"It may not have been hate. It may have been fear. I think she knew who killed Barry. I think that's what she wanted to tell me over the phone."

Dexter was silent for a long time, pondering. "This Mrs. Oliphant — the Hamiltons don't like her at all. What's your opinion?"

"She couldn't be nicer or more gracious to Joe and me. She makes us feel completely at home."

Dexter laughed. "I hate to shatter your girlish illusions, but your friend Maitland is the kind of man hostesses fight to get hold of."

"I suppose he is," I said in surprise.

This time Dexter leaned back in the seat and fairly roared with laughter. "Sue, you are wonderful. You are unique. The man is obviously nuts about you and . . ." He really let himself go this time.

"I don't see what is so funny. I like Joe. I think he's swell." I sounded cross but I couldn't help it. "And I don't think Mrs. Oliphant is interested in his income, whatever it is. There's not a vulgar or calculating streak in her."

"No?" His eyes were dancing.

"No. I think she's interested in the house next door because, whatever you may believe, she is convinced that someone there damned near killed her in mistake for Paula."

That silenced him, whether he took Mrs. Oliphant seriously or not. "Sue, I don't like this setup. I don't want you involved in all this ugliness. Go back home. After all, there is nothing you can accomplish here."

"I can find out what Paula wanted me to do. There was something that was desperately important to her. Something urgent."

He turned, his arm stretched across the back of the seat, and looked at me. "You are more like Paula than I had realized. You carry a job through, don't you?"

"I try."

He lifted my hand, kissed the palm lightly. "More power to you."

We had driven back through the village and were on the country lane when I said, "What do you really think of Warren King?"

"Back to him again? I don't, if I can help it. He's not the kind of person you think about. He's as completely negative as any man I ever encountered."

"I wonder."

95

"What on earth is this obsession with Warren King?"

"His open dislike of Paula; his hostility toward me."

"That's because of Paula's second will. He is going to fight to the death to prove unsound mind, you know. His reasons, I might point out, aren't like mine. He wants the Hamiltons, specifically Ruth, to have Barry's money."

"If I'm right, that's what Paula wanted too."

"But, my dear girl . . ."

"Look, Dexter, I knew my sister. She was married and divorced twice before she married Barry. Both men had a lot more money than he possibly could have had, and she refused any alimony. She wouldn't take a cent. Her character didn't change in the last three months of her life. If she altered her will, it must have been because she planned to start divorce proceedings against Barry. She never expected me to inherit the Hamilton money, and I might as well tell you right now I haven't the slightest intention of taking it."

"Then what did she expect?"

"That is what I intend to find out."

8

Dexter dropped me at the Oliphant house and then backed down the lane to the Hamilton driveway. Joe was with Mrs. Oliphant in her room. They were talking their heads off and drinking highballs.

Mrs. Oliphant broke off to wave to me. "Sit down, Sue. What would you like to drink?"

"Why this alcoholic binge at," I looked at my watch, "four thirty in the afternoon?"

"You and Joe are dining with the Hamiltons, and may God have mercy on your souls. You dine at six after one measly little vermouth. Hence the fortification."

"Is a Tom Collins legal at four thirty?"

"Don't be stuffy," Mrs. Oliphant told me severely and ordered the drink.

The room was shaded and cool with a heavenly breeze. Mrs. Oliphant moved restlessly and I knew that the cast must be uncomfortable though she made no complaint.

"And where," Joe demanded, "have you been? Another half hour and I'd have called out the state police." Somewhat to my surprise he was not joking.

"I've been for a ride with Dexter Webb."

"Now there's a man who doesn't let the grass grow under his feet," Mrs. Oliphant said with a laugh.

"It wasn't my charms. He could withstand them without any difficulty. He was helping me out of a nasty situation."

"Nasty?" Joe sat bolt upright.

"Luella." I described my encounters at the pool with Luella, Tommy, and Blanche. There wasn't anything I could see to cause Mrs. Oliphant's gales of laughter.

"My dear, I could hear them!"

"I can't help it. When I remember what people say I remember how they say it."

Mrs. Oliphant's gaiety slipped from her. "Do you think Luella is unbalanced?"

"It sounds to me," Joe said, "as though the woman is dangerous. My God! Implying that Paula killed Barry."

"Oh, Joe! If there's any dangerous potential in that lot, you'll find it in Blanche Hamilton. In my considered opinion, if you got in her way or took what she wanted, she would as soon stick a knife in you as not."

Mrs. Oliphant dropped her highball glass, which shattered on the floor. "You are quite right. I should have remembered before. It was in Egypt about four years ago. She killed her husband."

"Killed him!" Joe was startled.

"Well, that's what they said at first.

Anyhow, he got an overdose of sleeping pills. He was an appalling little man, deformed in some way, almost a dwarf, with a face like Silenus. He must have been twenty years older than she was. I think he had something to do with the government, but I'm vague about that. We didn't move in the same circles. Blanche had been seen around Cairo wearing a diamond necklace that made you need dark glasses. After a few days, it was discovered that her husband had committed suicide, or taken the stuff by accident. The papers sort of hinted. A little later, the wife of one of the government officials went around wearing a fabulous diamond necklace and Blanche faded out of the picture. I simply didn't realize who she was. All I knew was that she was familiar, that I had seen the woman somewhere before."

Carry brought my drink and cleared up the debris of Mrs. Oliphant's.

"So that," she exclaimed, "is why Blanche raised such a stink about my candid camera shots!" Then her jaw sagged.

"Hey, are you all right?" Joe asked anxiously.

"I told you I didn't see Barry's murderer. Now I wonder. The only person I saw leaving his study by that outside door on the afternoon of his death was Blanche Hamilton. Of course, I hadn't been watching the place all the time, whatever the Hamiltons think. I woke up from my nap and just before I went to take my bath I casually picked up the binoculars. She was standing there."

Joe was watching me. "Sue, what did Webb have to say about Luella's accusation while you were out with him?"

"He believed her." I told him of the quarrel Luella claimed to have overhead between Barry and Paula.

"Barry said, 'Paula! Oh, don't,' and then there was a blow. Is that the way it was? Damn it, Sue, Paula couldn't strike anyone!"

"That's what I think. Luella is a neurotic and jealous and vindictive. She's making the whole thing up."

"Mrs. Oliphant," Joe asked, "when you had your accident, how long was it after Barry's murder?"

"You'll have to check with Dr. Ames. He came to me from the Hamilton house."

"And Paula came running from her room when you fell?"

"No, she wasn't in her room. I'd sent Carry in to borrow the beach robe."

"Then you don't actually know where she was when her husband died?"

"No, but — don't try to confuse me, Joe. And why — with someone like Blanche Hamilton around, you look for anyone else . . ."

"I'm looking for someone, Mrs. Oliphant, but I'll take a specially good look tonight at Mrs. Tommy Hamilton."

11

"I wonder what it feels like to dine with a murderer," I said as Joe and I walked across the lawn and around to the front door of the Hamilton house.

Joe gripped my arm so hard he hurt me. "Look here, you've got to stop play-acting. You don't really believe in any of this. You are dramatizing. But this is for real. Don't stare at Blanche wondering if she is a killer. Don't open your trap any more than you have to. And for God's sake, Sue, be careful."

Never before had I heard that savage tone in his voice and I was so impressed that I agreed meekly to everything he said.

This time it was Mrs. Hamilton who admitted us, after calling nervously to make sure no reporter had slipped through the cordon. With Joe's sharp warning ringing in my ears I was careful not to stare at Blanche Hamilton, though when she offered that diamond-incrusted hand I thought this woman might have killed her husband, killed Barry, killed Paula.

I needn't have worried about betraying my interest in her. Except for a brief greeting she paid no attention to me at all and, as soon as the introductions had been performed, she cut Joe neatly out of the pack, drew him down on a love seat beside her and monopo-

101

lized him. It was as neat an operation as I had ever seen.

As Mrs. Oliphant had warned us, we were served a small glass of vermouth before going to the table. Mrs. Hamilton had cooked the dinner with Luella's help but it was Ruth who insisted on serving, which she did with an unnecessary degree of bustle and rushing back and forth.

Mrs. Hamilton had placed Joe at her right. "Just a simple home dinner," she told him. "We aren't attempting to entertain at this time."

"And, of course, we can't compete with the way Mr. Maitland lives," Luella said.

Even the doting Mrs. Hamilton must have felt that this went a bit beyond the bounds. Her round face flushed. "We felt so awful, so ashamed, when we heard that you had to go to Sarah Oliphant's, and this was Paula's home, after all. Of course, I can see why Sarah was so eager to have you, but it's absurd. Miss Wales — this is family, so we must call you Sue — you are to have Barry's room, and Dexter says that Mr. Maitland can have the spare bed in the guesthouse."

Overnight the Hamiltons seemed to have suffered a sea change in regard to me, or perhaps they simply couldn't bear the thought of our staying with Mrs. Oliphant.

I looked at Joe for orders. That's what his rage had reduced me to. He was looking

102

from face to face, his round eyes curiously intent.

"You are awfully kind," he said, "but we wouldn't dream of putting you to inconvenience and we are most comfortable where we are."

"Planning to stay long?" Warren King asked.

"It's hard to say. Actually I am a man who hates to make plans. I like lots of elbow room for action. My idea of the ultimate horror is one of those organized tours where you have to arrive at such a place at such a date and leave at such an hour. Suppose you want to linger. Suppose you discover a side road more interesting than the highway. I'm a creature of the moment."

Warren pondered this gravely and Tommy laughed. "Two minds that work alike. I knew I'd find you congenial. I like to pick up and go where and when I please."

"Go where?" Blanche asked.

"Whither thou goest, my love. I see you've been packing this afternoon. I nearly broke a toe on that big suitcase of yours."

"I was putting away some heavy clothes. I should have done it weeks ago." Blanche's eyes sought her young husband's and held them. He stirred uncomfortably.

Warren insisted on helping Ruth clear the table. Judging by her surprise, this domestic touch was somewhat out of his usual line. I couldn't help wondering whether Dexter had told him of my decision not to take Paula's money.

"No, you sit still," he told Luella, "you should rest. I understand you've been working all day on Barry's papers."

"Just the bills and unanswered letters that were in the desk drawer. Dex still has the keys to the files. I looked for you, Dex, but —"

"He took Miss Wales — our Sue — for a ride." Blanche smiled at Luella as though saying, "And I hope that hurts."

There was no getting away from the cosy family atmosphere. *Gemütlich* was the word for the Hamiltons.

Luella had managed to avoid speaking to me so far. Now she looked straight at me. "At first I thought you weren't at all like Paula. At least she was quite pretty — if you like that type. But you are like her, aren't you? You want to spoil things. She came here and spoiled everything. She never loved Barry, though he worshiped her. She just liked taking a man away from someone else. I'm the one who belonged here. She didn't. No one wanted her. I'm the one who helped Barry and typed his books and wrote his letters and everything. But nothing was the same after she came."

"Then why did you stay?" I asked in the stricken silence that followed her outburst.

104

"Because the Hamiltons wanted me. They needed me."

"Even Barry?" That was cruel but at the moment I didn't much care.

"I've always typed his books. No one else could read his handwriting. And then," slowly the blood surged over Luella's face, emphasizing the patches of eczema, "I began to build a new life. And she tried to destroy that too. She was bad. She killed Barry."

"No!"

To my surprise it was John Hamilton, the self-effacing, the ineffectual, who said sharply, "Luella, Sue is our guest. You don't know —"

Luella was completely beside herself and well into hysterics. "You'd be surprised at what I know. Yes, you'd be surprised. I know about those quarrels Barry had the day before he died. And I know what he planned to put in his next book if — someone — wasn't reasonable."

"Luella," Tommy said, "if you don't shut up I'll throttle you."

And on that note the simple home dinner broke up. Dexter rose nobly to the occasion and drew Luella away. Joe found himself cornered by the lawyer and gave me a look of comic resignation. And John Hamilton said in his gentle voice, "Let's talk, my dear," and led the way down the hall to a big, beautiful room, book-lined, with a handsome desk and

105

deep comfortable armchairs.

"This was my son's study." When he leaned back in his chair, eyes closed, I realized how frail he was, how unutterably weary, how futile. There was no strength in his face.

I looked around the room, which seemed unexpectedly familiar because it had been photographed so often. What took me by surprise was the long mirror set between two bookcases. The man must have been Narcissus. With that mirror there was no escaping his own image. Then I stared at it. No matter how absorbed Barry might have been it was most unlikely that he would not have seen his own murderer, watched the approach of his own murder. *Paula. Oh, don't.*

Without opening his eyes, Mr. Hamilton said, "I'm sorry, my dear. Sorry about that outbreak of Luella's. She's impossible, and a fool, of course. She pins her hopes on a quite unattainable dream and then falls apart when the dream doesn't materialize. For years she was in love with Barry. Eventually they drifted into a kind of engagement, chiefly because my wife was all for it. She thought Luella would be a perfect daughter-in-law, which is probably true. But a wife? No, it would never have worked. Luella would have bored Barry to death in a month."

His eyes were open now, watching me. "Barry loved Paula with all his heart. I'd

106

like you to know that."

"But something went wrong."

"Something went wrong. I don't know what. My son never confided in me. Not that we weren't friends but I was, after all, a dependent, a failure, not a man on whose judgement he could rely."

"Oh, surely . . ." I began in embarrassment.

He smiled, and I caught a glimpse of the resemblance between him and Barry, a trace of the famous Mona Lisa smile. On the whole, he said, he thought Barry had been right. He was not really a man of substance. Like Keats, his name was writ in water.

Keats then, not Shelley. My embarrassment ebbed. In a sense, the elder Hamilton had made a career of graceful failure. The gentle voice went on with a capsule story of his life. I got the impression that no one listened to him and he needed to talk. He had tried many things, both in business and the arts — he wasn't specific about what arts — but his soul was stifled by routine, by the dull day-to-day disciplines. A free spirit balked at being curbed.

It was a familiar story of failure, but the failure, in his eyes, had taken on a kind of nobility unsullied by the prosaic qualities that led to achievement. Listening to him, I wondered how much of all this he managed to believe, though I had learned to what extent

107

the average person succeeds in believing his own myths.

In a sense he answered my unspoken question. "It must have seemed to Paula when she married Barry that he bore a tremendous load, having his whole family dependent on him, but in a way he liked that. He was never as self-confident as people believed. He needed constant reassurance. And a family dependent on him, revolving around him —"

"Perhaps just an affectionate family who like being together," I said as tactfully as I could. "Anyhow, the Tommy Hamiltons weren't dependent." I broke off, realizing in dismay that my precarious tact had tripped me up as usual.

"Oh, yes." He ran his fingers up the leather arm of his chair. "Yes, Blanche is quite well off." He added in a burst of candor, "I have never understood why she goes on living in a country village. There is nothing for her here. And the local women — you know how women are — don't seem to take to her much. Matter of fact, Barry didn't like her either. He accepted the fact that Tommy was a drifter, the kind who would never carry his own weight. But Blanche — that marriage embarrassed Barry. It made Tommy look like a — a gigolo. Not long before he died, Barry admitted to me that he had told Tommy they ought to move on. New York perhaps. Florida. California. But now I don't suppose they'll leave." The prospect did not seem to please him.

He looked around the room. "You know, this is the first time I've been in here since Barry was found. I see they have removed all — it's very tidy. This was my son's sanctuary. I doubt if I spent an hour here in three months. He — very naturally, of course — didn't like interruptions."

I mentioned the outside door.

"Oh, yes, there were times when he had to get away, take a walk, something like that, but he didn't want to see people and break his line of thought. Of course, no one but Barry ever used that door."

I started to tell him that Mrs. Oliphant had seen Blanche coming out the afternoon of the murder. But what was the use? This ineffectual escapist would be of no help.

"Paula wasn't here, was she, when Barry died?"

"I never saw her after the murder was discovered. We were all in such a turmoil and there were so many people: the doctor, the police, and, when Luella found that the Masters script was missing, the newsmen. In droves."

"Who found Barry?"

"Luella. She had always given him a lot of help." Again that Mona Lisa smile curved his lips and I began to suspect that, after all, he observed a great deal that went on around

109

him; he simply withdrew from any responsibility for it. "More help than he wanted, I imagine, but Barry felt guilty about her, felt that he owed her something for those disappointed hopes. And then," this time the smile was deeper, "there is something a little intoxicating about the burning of incense.

"Well, Luella went into the study with some letters she had been typing for him and found him. She screamed and then called me and my wife and Tommy. Blanche was in her room asleep; we thought she was just taking a nap but we had trouble rousing her and learned later that she had taken a sleeping pill. She explained that she had been sleeping badly and she was trying to catch up.

"Then at last we found Ruth, who had been gathering wild flowers in those woods behind our property. She went to pieces and was quite hysterical. Then she pulled herself together and called the doctor. Paula was at Mrs. Oliphant's. Later I heard that when Dr. Ames went over there to set Mrs. Oliphant's leg he broke the news to Paula and she stayed and helped him with the cast. That was like her, you know. To put aside her own grief while she helped someone else."

"Then you don't believe Luella's story about hearing that quarrel with Barry when he was killed."

Poor old Mr. Hamilton was used to evasive action. He didn't like being cornered, forced

110

to take a stand. "I don't believe Paula killed Barry. But I don't believe either that Luella was lying. I think she misunderstood or misinterpreted what she heard."

"But she hasn't told the police?"

"It was Dr. Ames who notified the police. Luella knew then about the missing script and that bewildered us all. We simply didn't know what to think. We were so confused that it was hours before anyone thought of telling Dexter. By that time, of course, his office had closed for the day and he had, unfortunately, gone out to dinner. When we finally got hold of him he caught the first train up." Mr. Hamilton hesitated. "Train? No, I believe they don't run up here any more. A bus. They say the service is very good."

The door opened and Ruth looked in. When she saw us talking she frowned. "Father, you know you ought to be resting."

"Later." When she did not move he repeated, "Later, Ruth," and she closed the door.

As I started to get up he put his long thin hand on my arm. "Don't go. I so rarely have anyone to talk to. It's a great indulgence. Ruth is well-meaning but she doesn't listen. Tommy . . ." he dismissed Tommy with a gesture. "My wife finds any conversation that doesn't deal with domestic problems or personalities a waste of time. I miss Paula not only because she was so lovely to look at but

111

because she listened."

I couldn't help wondering if that was what Barry had wanted, too. A listener. Not conversation. A monologue addressed to an admiring audience.

For a moment I thought Mr. Hamilton had dozed off with the disconcerting abruptness of old age and then he said, "Are you comfortable at Sarah Oliphant's?"

"Very."

"I'm glad, you know, that Paula had her to go to when — after —" His fingers drummed on the chair arm. "I'll never understand that breakup. She and Barry never had a disagreement of any kind until the day before he died. I saw Paula when she came out of their room, a weekend bag in her hand. I'll never forget her as she was that day. Barry looked as though something in him had broken. He said, 'You don't realize what you are asking.' And Paula — so frozen, so white — saying, 'I'll be there for twenty-four hours, in case you change your mind.' And Barry said, 'But you won't change yours?' And Paula said, 'I can't.' There was something inexorable about her, something I had never expected existed. My son was self-centered, he was in some ways outrageously vain, but he was so madly in love with Paula that I believe he would have done anything — anything — to win her approval. If he had only been given time."

There was nothing I could say.

"I'm not sure she was made properly welcome here. There was Luella, of course, and then — somehow we had all settled on Barry, become too dependent, resentful of change. Now we've got to learn to stand on our own feet." This time, his smile, with the disconcerting way of family resemblances, was like Ruth's in a moment of martyrdom. "And high time, too," he said cheerfully. "Whatever our dreary friend Warren may say, I don't resent Paula's will. I have a curious faith in her — rightness." He stood up. "Perhaps I had better share you with the others. I have been selfish."

He took me back to the living room, which was in darkness. For a moment he paused in perplexity. Then we heard the record player. The last movement of the Beethoven *Eroica* was coming to an end. We groped our way out onto the dark lawn to join the rest of the party.

9

Mrs. Oliphant had given Joe a key to the front door. It was still early when we got back to the house, only nine thirty, but the evening had seemed unending.

"I'm going to bed," I said.

"Mrs. Oliphant promised there would be a gin and tonic waiting," Joe said. "A nice long cool nightcap, to take the taste of the evening out of our mouths."

I went into the kitchen with him while he mixed the drinks and told him of my talk with Mr. Hamilton. "Whatever happened, Paula issued an ultimatum with a twenty-four-hour limit. Mr. Hamilton is sure Barry would have given in, sooner or later. And he believed Luella was telling the truth about the quarrel she overheard, as far as she understood it."

" 'Paula. Oh, don't!' " Joe repeated thoughtfully. "You know I have an inkling —"

"Not tonight, Joe. I've had it."

The bed in my room had been turned down, a reading lamp beside it was lighted. In the small bathroom, which had been made out of a large closet, I showered and put on

114

a filmy nightgown and matching robe that Paula had sent me. As I pulled on the robe I began to sniff. There was a strong scent of perfume in the air. A heavy perfume. I sniffed again. Following my nose I investigated the closet where I had hung my scanty wardrobe. The smell was stronger here. In the bedroom it was so powerful it covered the sweet, light scent of the roses. And now I knew what it was. Blanche had used it tonight. The smell was so strong that I thought she must be in the room and turned the switch so the big ceiling lights went on. Of course she wasn't there.

I went through the closet and even looked in the bureau drawers. Someone had searched everything I possessed. In a panic I hunted for my big handbag but, though things had been moved around, my money and driving license and credit cards were still there.

My first reaction was one of fury, second was bewilderment. What on earth would the woman want of me? My third was an impulse to lock my door, surely an extraordinary thing to do as a guest in a private house. My fourth was to tell Joe.

For a moment my hand froze on the doorknob. I was afraid to go out, to leave the shelter of this room. I remembered that Mrs. Oliphant had pitched down the stairs. Then I flung open the door and tore down the stairs.

My bedroom slippers were soft satin and heelless but Joe heard me. He was at the living room door as I reached the bottom of the staircase. I flung myself at him.

What happened then was the shock of my life. Joe's arms went around me and his mouth came down on mine. It was he, finally, who released me with a breathless little laugh, though his eyes were watching me rather anxiously.

"I just — went up in smoke," I said in a tone of wonder.

"Gunpowder," Joe said, still in that breathless voice.

"Well, why," I asked furiously, "didn't you ever do that before?"

This time Joe held me crushed against him, muffling his gust of laughter against my throat. "Oh, Sue, my darling idiot, my precious fool!" His lips traveled over my throat, stopped abruptly. He set me on my feet at some distance from him. "The reason I didn't risk making love to you must be fairly obvious. Where I am concerned, I mean. And I didn't know — that is, I was willing to wait and see if you might . . ."

There was a growing confidence in his manner and I didn't like it at all. After three years of hopeless devotion there seemed to be a good chance that this pleasant state of things would come to an end unless I took a firm stand.

"I haven't made up my mind about you," I said coldly.

He grinned all over his homely face. "Come back here."

I went as meekly as Mary's little lamb but probably faster.

"My girl?"

Not being able to speak I nodded violently so our two heads bobbed around like a couple of balloons. You simply can't be romantic about Joe even when — well . . .

"And now, while I am still the perfect gentleman, I am going to march you back to your room. But next time you come falling into my arms wearing practically transparent —"

"Joe! That's why I came. Someone has been searching my room."

"Someone — what?"

"Well, Blanche Hamilton. I could smell her."

"Smell?"

"Her perfume, you dope."

He grabbed my hand and went up to my room with me. The perfume was already fading. The room looked orderly enough.

"You're not dramatizing?"

"I'm not dramatizing. And I don't like it. Not one bit. And why? What was the woman looking for? What have I got that would interest her?"

"You forget that this was Paula's room. Tomorrow I'll ask Mrs. Oliphant who removed her things and we'll take this room apart until we find what someone was looking for. And you should go through Paula's things anyhow, don't you think? Her clothes and letters and personal belongings."

"I suppose so but I hate it. Like eavesdropping on the dead. And don't say someone; say Blanche. But what I can't see is how she managed it. Weren't you all together while Mr. Hamilton and I were talking in Barry's study?"

"Why yes, we — I suppose it's possible. It was dark as the hinges of hell out there on the lawn. No moon. They had turned out the living room lights so as not to attract bugs."

"Whose idea was that?"

"Tommy's. Then they put on that record, the Beethoven Third. Ruth said it would be a kind of requiem to Barry, the funeral march part, you know, so we all sat in solemn silence."

"The whole time?"

"Well, people went in and out unobtrusively, now and then. In my coarse way I assumed they were answering the call of nature, but I didn't inquire."

"You surprise me."

"Shut up, wench," Joe said absently. "Hey, get your toothbrush and whatever else you need. You're going to sleep in my room."

"I'm —"

118

"And no lascivious thoughts from you. I, like one of those tiresome saints, will take up my rest alone on this bed of nails. If any more night prowlers come around I prefer to deal with them myself."

He opened the door of his room, switched on the lights, removed his night gear. The oaf didn't even kiss me. He closed the door and I heard the key turn in the lock.

As I ran in fury to the door he whispered mockingly, "Don't make any noise. You'll disturb Mrs. Oliphant."

He went downstairs and I wondered what he was up to. A few minutes later he returned and I heard the pleasant sound of ice tinkling against a glass. I might have known.

I got into bed and settled back against the pillows, prepared to meditate dreamily about what had happened to me. Me! Going up in flames because Joe had kissed me. It was practically earth-shaking. Instead, I fell sound asleep.

II

The screams tore ragged holes in the silence of the night. I found myself sitting bolt upright in bed, my heart hammering. The sounds were coming from outside and I ran to the window. Light spilled out onto the lawn from Barry's study where the draperies were

119

wide open. Inside, people were moving around, lights were going on upstairs.

I caught up my robe and ran to the door. Then I remembered and banged on it. "Joe!" I shouted. "Joe, let me out!"

Mrs. Oliphant said in a startled voice, "Sue, what's wrong?" and I realized she did not know of the change of rooms. What she must be thinking of us! Well, Joe would have to clear my reputation.

No sleepless lover he, thinking how lucky he was to have won his girl. He slept like a log. I yelled again before I could waken him.

"Huh? What?" Then I heard his feet hit the floor. "Sue! You all right?"

"Let me out, you lug! Something is happening over at the Hamiltons'. They are screaming like air-raid sirens."

"So are you." He unlocked my door, tying the belt of his robe, red hair standing on end. "What goes on?"

"Sue!" Mrs. Oliphant called and I tapped on her door. "Come in. What's wrong?"

"Joe locked me in." I explained about changing rooms and told her why.

"Your room was searched this evening?" Like Jesting Pilate she did not stay for an answer. "What's going on next door?"

Joe helped her pull herself higher in bed, dragging the heavy cast, and piled pillows behind her. Then he abandoned her heartlessly and went to the window where he had

120

a box seat. I nudged him to make room for me.

Barry's study was like a lighted stage. Four people seemed to stand there frozen. Then a fifth appeared. Dexter clad in pajamas and robe. Dexter looking around. Dexter looking down. Dexter making a quick horrified gesture as though he rejected what he saw.

"What is it?" Mrs. Oliphant demanded. "For God's sake, what is it?"

"I can't tell. Seems to be an accident. I'm going over."

"I'm going with you."

"No," Joe said firmly.

He went hurling down the stairs with me at his heels, out of the house, across the lawn to the break in the hedge. Outside the Hamilton house he stubbed his toe on a garden chair, swore, limped on.

We stood looking in the long windows. Ruth, the only one fully dressed, was dialing a number. The others, the older Hamiltons, the Tommy Hamiltons, and Dexter, stood staring at the quiet figure sprawled on the floor. It was Luella, a scarf imbedded in her neck, and she was dead. I clutched at Joe's arm.

"Go back," he ordered me. "Keep out of this." He turned the knob of the study door, which opened at his touch, and I followed him in. No one even noticed us. If there is such a thing as collective shock, the Hamiltons were in it.

Ruth set down the telephone. "He's not there," she said blankly. "He's not there."

"His answering service should be on the job."

"Answering service?" She was still blank, as though the words did not register.

"Aren't you calling Dr. Ames?"

"I'm calling Warren."

"Oh, for God's sake!" Tommy said. "It's not a lawyer we need. It's a doctor."

"Sure about that?" Blanche rasped.

Joe took a hand. "You don't need a doctor," he said flatly. "The girl is dead."

Even at that unlikely moment Tommy took time off for a leisurely look at what my more or less diaphanous clothing revealed.

Mrs. Hamilton knelt beside the body. She was the only one to display any grief. "Oh, Luella!" she moaned, and reached out to the scarf.

"Don't touch her," Tommy said. "Don't touch anything. The girl has been murdered. You'll have to leave this room so as not to disturb anything. Sue, call the police." He acted like a top sergeant but no one seemed to object. While I made the call, he watched them file past him and down the hall to the living room.

"Oh, dear!" Mrs. Hamilton exclaimed. "The police again! What will the neighbors think of us?" With which piece of imbecility she sank into a chair, sobbing. Mr. Hamilton

122

had collapsed. His eyes were closed, his lips blue, his color terrible. Dexter took his wrist, felt for his pulse. He caught my eyes and his lips shaped the words, "Dr. Ames. Quick."

Aside from the private telephone in Barry's study there was one for family use in the hall. From there I called the doctor and told him what had happened, speaking in as low a voice as possible. He gave a horrified exclamation.

"We've already called the police. We don't need you for Luella. It's Mr. Hamilton. He looks awful."

"Fifteen minutes," the doctor said laconically.

Police sirens could be heard in the distance, swelling, coming nearer. Then we could see the big roof lights flashing. Car doors slammed.

Joe gave a questioning look at Tommy but he was lighting a cigarette for his wife. That was the limit of his self-imposed responsibilities. Ruth stared blindly at her shoes. So Joe admitted the police himself and led them back to the study.

There were more cars now, more men tramping down the hall, a good deal of low-voiced talk, and then, inevitably, the newsmen, baying like hounds on the scent.

At a word from Blanche, Tommy went into the hall where we could hear his voice raised in protest. At length a policeman was posted at the door to keep out intruders. I watched Mr. Hamilton, whose breathing alarmed me, so when the police took Dr. Ames to the study I cried out, "She doesn't need him now. Mr. Hamilton needs him."

"Dr. Ames is the doctor used by the police in Stockford," Blanche explained. "Autopsies and all that." She added dryly, "The Hamiltons have been through this twice before."

There was nothing we could do but wait. Oddly enough, no one asked the normal questions: How did it happen? Who could have done this? Who found her? Who screamed? They just sat and waited. Mr. Hamilton had not opened his eyes and I didn't even know whether or not he was conscious. His wife sobbed convulsively, but that didn't mean much. A sentimental woman, but not one of deep feelings.

Ruth stared at her shoes. Blanche pleated the exquisite white velvet of her robe, smoothed it out, pleated it. Tommy watched her with a curious expression. Dexter leaned against the wall. Once he looked at me and made a faint gesture indicating "chin up" but he wasn't able to produce even a reasonable facsimile of a smile.

The first person to come in was Dr. Ames, stooping with weariness. Automatically he straightened, as though prepared to shoulder someone else's burden, which was, I suppose,

124

the pattern of his life, and took a swift look around. He went straight to Mr. Hamilton. For a moment he looked down at him and then he went out to the telephone, pausing to speak to the policeman at the door. I heard him say, "Hospital — ambulance — oxygen — positively no questions now."

And still we waited. The ambulance had come and gone, taking the white-faced Mr. Hamilton, the doctor following in his car. After some prodding, Mrs. Hamilton had gone upstairs to fill a small bag for her husband. The usually and articulately helpful Ruth was unmoving, apathetic.

At length there were heavy footsteps in the hallway. Joe, realizing what the little procession meant, leaped for the door but not until we were all aware that Luella was leaving the house.

At last two men came in. The older one introduced himself as Lieutenant Graby. The young sergeant was named Knight. They were quiet and courteous but they were watchful. After all, this was the third time they had come to the Hamilton house to investigate a violent death.

While the sergeant opened his notebook the lieutenant asked, "Who was she?"

"Luella Matthews," Tommy said. "An old friend of the family."

"Any family of her own?"

"Not that we know of. She never mentioned anyone. She lived with us for three or four years."

"Who found her?"

There was a moment of uneasy silence. Then Ruth said, "I went to the study. I wanted to read my brother's book and I knew there should be a carbon in his files. My sister-in-law was there. She screamed as I came in."

The lieutenant looked thoughtfully at Ruth who was still wearing the cheap thin black linen dress she had worn at dinner. His eyes shifted to Blanche in her white velvet robe, which must have cost at least three hundred dollars.

"I had gone in just seconds ahead of Ruth," Blanche said. "I couldn't sleep so I was looking for something to read." Tommy gave his wife a surprised look. "Just as Ruth came in, I caught sight of Luella's body and screamed."

"Was Miss Matthews looking for a book too?" the lieutenant asked politely.

"Luella helped my son with his work," Mrs. Hamilton told him. "She had been trying to clear up his papers and accounts, working all day, ever since you people unlocked the study."

Joe's round eyes had been traveling from face to face. Now he noticed that the young sergeant was looking me over. He didn't like that at all.

126

"We heard the screams," he said, "and came running. This is Miss Wales, the sister of Mrs. Barry Hamilton. My name is Maitland. We are staying next door with Mrs. Oliphant. Perhaps, if you have any questions for Miss Wales, you will save them for later."

The lieutenant nodded, Joe jerked his head toward the door with all the courtly grace of a charging bull, and I obeyed without protest.

I dressed quickly, surprised to realize how cold I was, and pulled on a sweater. As Mrs. Oliphant's door was wide open and her lights were on, I looked in.

"Sue! I've been going crazy. What is happening over there? I heard sirens. Is there a fire? And me with my leg in a cast."

"Luella has been murdered; strangled. And Mr. Hamilton collapsed. I think it's his heart. He has gone to the hospital." Curled up at the foot of her bed I told her what had happened. "I called the police and Joe stayed over there. The Hamiltons have just fallen apart, so he sort of took over. He sent me back here."

She looked at me in disbelief. "It's horrible. Barry and Paula and now Luella. But why? Why?"

I shook my head. Even in the sweater I shivered though the night was warm. I kept seeing Luella's congested face.

"You had better get a good stiff drink, and,

127

Sue, I'm not being silly, I hope, but please make sure the doors are locked."

I went down to test the doors but I didn't pour myself a drink. As I explained to Mrs. Oliphant, it wouldn't do for the police to find me smelling like the face on the bar-room floor.

"If you expect the police to question you tonight," she said, "you had better wake Carry and ask her to fix some coffee and sandwiches. And a tray of drinks, if they are allowed to drink on duty. And, Sue, please bring me that blue bed jacket and my mirror."

"Shouldn't you rest? They won't disturb you."

"Don't be ridiculous. I can't rest with all this going on."

It wasn't necessary to awaken Carry. I made sandwiches, wrapped them in wax paper, and measured coffee, glad to have something to do. Back in Mrs. Oliphant's room I stood at the window. Lights still poured from Barry's study. In fact, the whole house was a blaze of light. Cars arrived, doors slammed, voices called. Once, incongruously, there was a laugh. The newshounds were out in force, but what anyone found to laugh at I couldn't imagine.

10

It was nearly three o'clock when Joe returned to the house, accompanied by the lieutenant and the sergeant. At Mrs. Oliphant's urgent request they came rather tentatively up to her bedroom.

Joe looked at my properly clad figure with approval and relief. There was no doubt about it, the halcyon days were over. He was going to be one of those husbands who Give Orders. If I hadn't fallen so devastatingly in love with the man, I'd have fought back.

"You look exhausted," Mrs. Oliphant said. "We have a tray of sandwiches and coffee for you in the dining room."

The tired faces lighted. "That's mighty nice of you," Graby said.

"If," I suggested, "Joe would bring up the tray we could talk and eat at the same time."

"Nice people don't do that," Joe remarked. "Before I marry you —"

"The tray," I reminded him. "On your way, Buster."

With the sergeant's help I cleared a table. When Joe had deposited the tray I poured coffee and he passed sandwiches.

129

"There are drinks down on the sideboard," Mrs. Oliphant told the men, "and an ice bucket."

"It's pretty late for that," Graby said regretfully, "but thank you, ma'am. We still have to get back and report. We won't keep you long. Just a couple of questions. But Mr. Maitland seemed to think —"

"What I think," Joe said, "is that it is time for us to pass on every crumb of information we have. The whole works. You first, Sue."

"No, first, what has happened over there?"

"They are going to bed," the lieutenant said. "We've finished for the night. But tomorrow, of course, we'll have to question them all again."

"You didn't find out anything?" I was incredulous.

"When they've had some rest we may get some sense out of them. What gets me is that Hamilton was the kind of guy who made a lot of enemies but this Matthews girl doesn't seem to have had any outside life at all."

"We don't think she was killed by an outsider," Joe told him. "We don't think these murders had anything to do with politics in general or Eliot Masters in particular. They were an inside job."

"Yeah?" The lieutenant was much too tired and harassed to have patience with the theories of amateurs.

"You speak your piece," Joe instructed me,

130

"and don't dramatize."

I started with Paula's telephone call after Barry's death and went on to her second will and Warren King's anger over it, and to her estrangement from Barry. This brought a startled exclamation from the lieutenant.

"That's true," Mrs. Oliphant assured him. "Mrs. Hamilton moved over here the day before she and her husband died. I had the definite impression that the marriage was breaking up."

"But no one said a thing, not even when she committed suicide." The lieutenant was frankly unbelieving.

"When she was murdered," I said crisply. I went on to tell him about my encounters with Luella and Tommy and Blanche at the swimming pool. When a grin plastered itself on the lieutenant's face and the sergeant's shoulders heaved, I realized I had caught their inflections again, but I couldn't help it. At least I had no difficulty in holding my audience. Then I went on to the simple home dinner and Luella's hysterical outburst.

"She knew about all the quarrels Mr. Hamilton had had?"

I nodded emphatically.

"And this Tommy Hamilton actually said he would throttle her?"

"It wasn't like that," Joe put in. "Oh, he used the expression, yes. I hold no brief for the egregious Tommy but it was more like

131

someone saying, 'I hope you choke.' One of those things. Not lethal."

"And he said his wife was packing?"

When both Joe and I agreed, the lieutenant asked Mrs. Oliphant's permission to use her telephone, called the Hamilton house, and instructed the man he had left on guard to look for a suitcase which Mrs. Thomas Hamilton had packed. While we waited, the two men had more coffee and dealt with the sandwiches. Then the policeman next door called back to report that there was no evidence of packing in Mrs. Thomas Hamilton's room and that her husband had shown him the luggage in the attic. All of it was empty.

"Then she lied about storing away her winter clothing," I said. I finished my account with the discovery that my room had been searched that evening and smelling Blanche's perfume. "And I guess that is all. The rest is really Mrs. Oliphant's story."

"I don't like this, lieutenant," she said in distress. "I don't really know anything except that someone threw me downstairs in mistake for Paula Hamilton and broke my leg. The rest is just hearsay and gossip."

The lieutenant set his cup down hard on its saucer and the sergeant's pencil ran straight off the notebook.

"Just a minute, ma'am. About this accident of yours."

"It was no accident, except that they got

132

the wrong person." She explained about wearing Paula's robe.

"And just a little while after that," I put in, "Paula called me, wanting desperately to tell me something, and she broke off when she was interrupted —"

"And that, lieutenant, is why we don't think an outsider killed these people," Joe concluded.

II

There was an odd expression on Lieutenant Graby's face. He shook his head as though trying to clear it. "I figured Mr. Maitland had something in mind but I wasn't prepared to have the applecart upset. Now as I understand it all three of you believe —"

"But we don't know," Mrs. Oliphant told him. "This thing is much too serious for speculation and guesswork."

"I think you can rely on us to sort it out, to weigh the evidence."

Mrs. Oliphant wasn't a lighthearted sixty now. She looked seventy, her face sagging with weariness and pain and anxiety. "But that's just it. I have no evidence." At his insistence, she made a despairing gesture of surrender and told the story of Blanche's arrest in Egypt for the murder of her husband by sleeping pills, her release, and the appearance of her fabulous necklace on the wife of a government official. No, she couldn't remember what her married name had been. When she had first met Mrs. Tommy Hamilton, she had realized that she had seen her somewhere before but she couldn't place her.

"And then," she indicated her camera, "I took some pictures of the Hamiltons: Paula because she was so beautiful and the rest for reasons of tact. As a rule, people seem to like to have their pictures taken, like writing their names on walls to prove they have been there. But Blanche was furious. She made a terrific scene and even demanded that I destroy my camera and give her the film. I refused to destroy the camera, but I did say I'd give her the picture I had taken of her. However, I had one shot of which I had great hopes, a tricky moonlight picture, so I refused to surrender the whole works. I really meant to give her that picture but a few days later Barry was killed and that same day I was laid up, so I never got around to it."

At her direction I found some slides and a small viewer on a bookshelf. Mrs. Oliphant examined them first and then passed them from hand to hand. The first was a full moon seen through mist. There followed the pictures of Paula and Barry I had seen in the *Times*, Mr. and Mrs. Hamilton look like Jack Sprat and his wife, Ruth walking across the lawn. Warren, Tommy, and Dexter had been taken on the edge of the pool. Tommy was trying to stand on his hands. Dexter had poised to dive. Warren looked as though he were waiting for someone to tell him whether the water was too cold.

Luella and Blanche had each been snapped on the terrace. Luella sat with her ankles neatly crossed, smiling as winningly as she could, poor thing, the scarred side of her face turned away from the camera. I remembered my last sight of her, the bulging eyes, the . . .

Joe was beside me, my hand tight in his. "She never felt a thing," he assured me. "It was over in a flash."

The lieutenant started to speak, caught Joe's glare, and subsided.

The last slide was of Blanche, her solid body half out of the chair as she started toward Mrs. Oliphant, one hand raised in protest, her lips drawn back as though she were about to bite.

"She sure didn't want that picture taken," the lieutenant agreed. "I'd like to borrow this, if I may. You'll get it back."

"I never want to see it again," Mrs. Oliphant told him. "Never."

"Anything else you think isn't evidence?"

"Well, I saw Blanche coming out of Barry's study the afternoon he was killed."

His mouth opened, closed. He swallowed hard. "I understood that no one but Mr.

Hamilton ever used that door, that it was kept locked."

"I saw her myself."

"What time was this?"

"Midafternoon, I think, perhaps later."

"Hamilton's body was found at five o'clock. He hadn't been dead long when Dr. Ames saw him." Graby looked at his notes. "About that outside door —"

"It wasn't locked tonight," I said. "Joe and I just walked in."

"And Mrs. Thomas Hamilton was right on the spot again," the lieutenant said thoughtfully.

"But so was Ruth," I pointed out, "and Ruth was the only one still dressed. Oh, of course, Blanche must have wanted to find out about Barry's next book. That's what Luella said. You remember, Joe? She said she was the only one who knew what Barry's next book was to be about, unless someone was reasonable. And that's when Tommy said he would throttle her."

The lieutenant pushed back his chair. "The best teacher of crime detection I ever had told me never to take anything for granted, to check and double-check. We've loused this up badly. We took for granted that Hamilton's murder was political, that his wife killed herself for grief."

He had a disarming smile. "You've given me a lot to think about and a lot of head-

136

aches." He stood up. "There's nothing else you've kinda sorta thought of but didn't mention?" The lieutenant had fallen for Mrs. Oliphant too.

"Nothing." She was positive.

He looked at me.

"Well, there are the sleeping pills. I can't help wondering about them because they do keep cropping up, don't they? Blanche's first husband — at least another husband died of an overdose of sleeping pills; Blanche took sleeping pills and went out like a light right after Barry was found. Surely they don't work that fast."

"There could be a nice case built around Mrs. Thomas Hamilton," Graby said. "But we need something to hold it together."

"Like what?" I asked.

"Like," he said, "a motive."

11

The morning was hot and sultry with a yellow, sullen sky, and the air heavy to breathe. Even a cold shower failed to refresh me or the chilled cantaloupe and shirred eggs and English muffins Carry served me at a little table under a tree on the lawn. Fortunately it was on the side away from the Hamilton house. I knew by Carry's expression that she had heard of the murder. As a matter of fact, she could not have escaped the murder. The news was the first thing I heard on the little transistor radio beside my bed. And it was still political.

Whatever new line the police might be following, they had released no information beyond the fact that the dead girl had been Barry Hamilton's secretary.

Eliot Masters had been interviewed and had expressed his horror at the crime. A woman whose dubious profession was forecasting the future said that she had foretold the Hamilton murders some months earlier and added, for good measure, that there would be another death.

Personal friends of Barry Hamilton, at least people who claimed that they had been per-

138

sonal friends, related anecdotes about him, none of which had any point except to indicate that the narrator had been there.

Miss Sue Wales, actress, sister of Mrs. Barry Hamilton, whose suicide had followed the discovery of her husband's death, had called the police when the murder of Miss Matthews was discovered.

Joseph Wentworth Maitland, who had accompanied Miss Wales from Pennsylvania where she was appearing with the Lenox Stock Company had, like his famous taciturn maternal grandfather, Hayes Wentworth, refused to make any public statement. The Wentworths — here, for lack of any fresh news, the commentator in desperation gave a dreary account of the career of Hayes Wentworth. As the man had been dead for twenty years and he had been usually disagreeable, it was hard to inject any particular drama into this.

There were police cars at the Hamilton house again and a man stationed outside to turn back newsmen and sightseers. Mr. Maitland, Carry said, had breakfasted some time ago. I wasn't surprised when I discovered, after a look at my watch, that it was nearly eleven o'clock. Mrs. Oliphant, the housekeeper said, had asked for her tray an hour ago and then had gone back to sleep. She looked just awful.

In spite of her wistful expression I didn't

talk to her about what had happened the night before. When I had slept at all I had dreamed horribly. Luella, with a swollen and blackened face, was chasing me, and my feet were rooted. I couldn't run. After the first nightmare I deliberately tried to stay awake, but I slept again and I dreamed again. And always it was I who was the victim, I who was afraid.

Mrs. Oliphant was still resting, her door closed, when I had dawdled over breakfast as long as I could. Then, as there was still no sign of Joe and no message from him, I left him a brief note, told Carry I wouldn't be there for lunch, collected my handbag, and set out briskly for the village.

This, as I realized belatedly, meant passing the Hamilton house and the line of newsmen's cars, which were roped off beyond the property. As I walked past I was surrounded. I was Miss Wales, wasn't I? I was Mrs. Barry Hamilton's sister? I had been the one to call the police last night? Was Mr. Maitland co-operating with the police?

I remembered Dexter's words, said, "No comment," and went on hastily, trying to shield my face from the cameras with my large and cumbersome handbag.

In the village proper I had no difficulty in finding a florist. There was only one and his shop was conveniently located, as a kind of way station, between the hospital and an impressive old Colonial home that turned out to be an undertaking parlor.

Carrying the flowers I entered the small and unexpectedly attractive waiting room of the hospital. Mr. Hamilton, I was told after the operator checked by telephone, had rested comfortably and he could receive visitors. From her inquiry it was apparent that I was the first person to display any interest in the poor old man.

When I had given the flowers to a floor nurse, I found Mr. Hamilton alone in a two-bed room, propped up on pillows. Perhaps he had rested well but there was no indication of it. His color was better than it had been the night before and his breathing was normal, but his eyes were sunken, they looked like deep pits in his face.

He brightened when he saw me. "Sue, how nice of you!" Then his face stiffened. "Everything all right?" He recognized the inanity of this. "I mean — nothing more has happened?"

"No, I just came to see how you are. Last night I was worried about you. The shock was too much for you."

"The shock, yes." He closed his eyes.

The nurse bustled in with the vase of flowers. "Well," she said with dreadful cheerfulness, "looks as though a certain young lady thinks a lot of you!" She gave us both a coy smile and went out.

Seeing his expression I giggled. "Go ahead and say it. You'll feel better."

He chuckled and seemed to relax, groped under his pillow and grunted with annoyance. "My wife forgot handkerchiefs."

I found him some tissues and promised to deliver handkerchiefs from the house.

"What happened after I went into that faint or whatever it was?" His eyes forbade me to say what it was. "I've tried to piece it together. But what with the patient in the next bed dying during the night and the stuff Dr. Ames gave me, I don't seem to be able to understand it."

"Personally," Blanche said from the doorway, "I don't see why you shouldn't know about it. If it were me, I'd simply crawl up the walls until I found out, but — so far — no one really knows."

She raised her eyebrows in acknowledgment of my presence, raised them higher over the flowers, came to sit beside the bed, so close that I had to draw my own chair out of the way.

"Luella is dead, isn't she? I got that right?"

"She was strangled," Blanche told him, "but so far that's all the police know."

He wasn't really relaxed at all. He was tense and he was watching her the way a snake watches a bird.

"No clues?" For a moment there was the shadow of the Mona Lisa smile. "I thought there were always clues," he said. And watched her.

"Nothing at all."

The lines around his mouth seemed to relax.

"But our Sue is spreading quite a story, you know. According to her, just a few minutes after Barry was murdered, Mrs. Oliphant was thrown downstairs and broke her leg. Someone, our Sue believes, mistook her for Paula whose robe she was wearing. One of the Hamiltons, according to our Sue, killed Barry and Paula and Luella."

"Out!" Dr. Ames said in a tone I had not heard him use before. He pressed the button for the nurse, adjusted his stethoscope. "What kind of trick do you think you are playing? This man has a bad heart, Any shock — out!" As a nurse appeared he said, "See that Mrs. Hamilton is not admitted again. Under any circumstances. Now get me . . ."

II

Blanche and I did not leave the hospital together. I loitered in the lobby until she was out of sight.

Back at Mrs. Oliphant's I stopped in for a minute to see how she was. In a becoming soft rose bed jacket, her hair beautifully arranged, she appeared to have survived the night in a much less battered condition than

I had. She hadn't heard from Joe except that he wouldn't be in for lunch. I told her about my visit to Mr. Hamilton at the hospital and Blanche's gaffe.

"You know I wouldn't have believed your nice Dr. Ames could be so angry."

"But what was the woman trying to do? She must have known that in John's condition he shouldn't be told anything that might upset him."

From the vantage point at her window I was able to inform her that the police cars had gone. One man was still on duty, holding off sightseers. Another stood at the door, and yet the murderer must be someone inside.

"What are you going to do this afternoon?" Mrs. Oliphant asked.

"I promised to pick up some handkerchiefs for Mr. Hamilton, and, sooner or later, I'll have to go through Paula's things. The longer I wait, the harder it will be."

Everything in me rebelled at the idea of entering the house next door again but there was no help for it. The policeman took my name. It was Dexter who admitted me.

From the living room I could hear the sound of hysterical sobbing. "That's Ruth," Dexter said in a low tone. "She's been going on like that for hours. She wasn't all that fond of Luella. If Warren can't manage her I'll have to call Dr. Ames again."

"Again?"

"Yes, I had the poor devil back here at four o'clock this morning when Mrs. Hamilton went to pieces. He put her under sedation. Now it's Ruth." He rubbed his tired face. "Thank heaven, Warren showed up at last. I thought that would do the trick, but she's been at him and at him about where he was last night, why he didn't answer his telephone. I hope he has sense enough to realize what he'd be letting himself in for if he married her, even if she does get a slice of Barry's money."

Hearing the tight edge of exhaustion in his voice I said, "I don't believe you've slept at all."

"Sleep! I've forgotten what the word means. God, what a situation. Luella of all people! Now if it had been —" The words stopped as though a hand had been shoved over his mouth, and I saw Blanche coming down the stairs.

"You again," she said with the warm cordiality that stamped the Hamiltons.

"Mr. Hamilton wants some handkerchiefs." I waited and so did she.

"Tommy can take them to the hospital. Thanks."

"And I'd like to go through Paula's things. I don't want to be a nuisance at a time like this but I suppose it has to be done."

"Come along." She turned back up the stairs. The room Barry and Paula had shared

145

was above the study, with the same spacious dimensions, the same luxury. "I picked up the stuff Paula had left at Sarah Oliphant's and brought it back here. We didn't want any more scandal. After all, this was supposed to be where she lived."

"According to Mrs. Oliphant you brought it back right away."

"The next morning. Her suicide was bad enough without —"

"After Luella's murder can you still claim that Paula killed herself?"

"After Luella's murder," Blanche said in her rasping voice, "I'm not making any claims. It's not healthy. And that goes for you too."

"Not," I agreed, "with a murderer in the house. Thank you, Blanche. I can handle this alone." I practically closed the door in her face.

I should have known, of course. There were two suitcases on one of the twin beds and, unless Blanche had simply stuffed Paula's clothes into them, the bags had been ransacked. I took out everything, sorted the dresses and undies, pajamas and shoes, a handbag and a small cardboard accordion file. Then I went through the clothes carefully, looked in pockets, put them to one side to be given to some charitable organization. I hunted through the pockets of the suitcases, and, feeling rather silly, looked for false bottoms, though I probably wouldn't have known one if I had seen it.

That left the handbag and the small file. The handbag held the usual accumulation a woman seems to need: handkerchief, cosmetics, keys, cigarette case and lighter, check book showing a balance of $4,500, a billfold containing about $30 and the usual cards people require: identification, social security, insurance, credit. In one pocket there were two snapshots, one of Barry and one of me. In the other were her car registration, driver's license, and pilot's license.

The file was my last hope. It held neatly filed canceled checks, tax records, receipted bills, and an address book. And that was that.

I looked down at the little heap of things on the bed, just enough to fill two suitcases, all that remained of Paula, the only record she had left of her restless and tormented life.

Somehow I didn't believe it. I came to a perfectly irrational conclusion. Paula had left me a message. The fault was mine that I had failed to find it. One thing seemed certain. I would not find it in this big beautiful bedroom, which bore no trace of Paula's presence. I opened the closets. One of them held a number of men's suits, polished shoes carefully treed, hats on a shelf above. The other contained evening dresses and some negligees which were much more elaborate than Paula's usual taste, and a fur coat in a sealed

147

bag. These, I guessed, had been Barry's gifts and she had left them behind. To me that was the most eloquent evidence of a rupture between them that I could find. With his lavish gifts she had rejected all that was Barry.

I returned to the small bundle on the bed. Paula hadn't gathered much moss in her life. Carrying her handbag and the little file I went out of the room and closed the door gently. In the living room Ruth and Warren were still quarreling. In the study Dexter was taking down what I took to be large leather-bound books. He saw me and waved for me to come in.

"Anything?" he asked, as I placed Paula's handbag and the little file on the desk.

I shook my head. "What are you doing with those impressive volumes?"

"These are Barry's files. Handsome, aren't they?" Each one, I saw, was actually a metal box, and on the back, in gold, was the title of an eighteenth century theologist.

"It was a good way of preventing people from looking at them."

"What on earth did he keep there?"

"I don't know yet. I hope to find carbon copies of his last book and some clue as to what the next one was to be about."

"But surely this isn't up to you! Can't Warren handle things?"

A tired grin flickered over Dexter's face.

"Aside from the fact that I am consumed with curiosity, it strikes me that Warren has his hands full, clearing himself with Ruth."

"You look exhausted, Dexter."

"I am. The police were back this morning and they will keep coming back. And back. And back. Today they were after the Tommy Hamiltons. Tomorrow it will be someone else. And meanwhile the work at the office is accumulating, stuff I can't delegate to anyone now that Paula isn't there. But why, for God's sake, why did someone want to strangle Luella? If it had been Blanche —"

"Yeah?" Tommy walked into the study, his face still wearing that boyish look, his body taking a boyish stance, but his eyes were cold. "Suppose you leave my wife out of this, Dex. Because I'm warning you, one more crack and you won't know what hit you."

"Calm down," Dexter said wearily.

"Who set the police to checking on Blanche and me by the dawn's early light?" In answer to his own question Tommy's eyes traveled to me, rested speculatively. "So that's it. Little Miss Fixit. You're the blabber-mouth."

"Tommy, you really are making a fool of yourself."

Tommy ignored him. "You keep your cute little nose where it belongs." As he came farther into the room I scrambled to my feet.

"I'll be at Mrs. Oliphant's," I told Dexter

149

with as much dignity as I could summon up, "if anyone wants me."

"No one will," Tommy said, "except for your tame moneybags. Keep your hooks in him, Gypsy Girl, and get them out of us."

"Then you had better tell your wife not to try to shock your father into another heart attack," I said, suddenly furious, and I ran past him.

Because the argument still raged in the living room between Ruth and Warren, I found my way back to the door that opened on the terrace. Seeing the pool I remembered Luella swimming up and down. The air was sultry and oppressive as though a storm was brewing somewhere. I couldn't sit still. I was as restless as a cat. To go back to the village I'd have to brave the newsmen again. Joe wasn't home. Mrs. Oliphant was resting.

Behind the little guesthouse were woods. The trees were not high, practically all second growth, but the underbrush was thick. Someone had beaten a path through it, a shady friendly path, and I began to follow it, wondering if this was where Barry had walked while he polished up the poison darts he threw into his victims' defenseless backs.

First, it was just a kind of vibration, then a snapping twig, then an uneasy sensation between my shoulder blades. Someone was following me. Someone who didn't call and ask me to wait. Someone then, who wasn't

150

friendly. I wanted to run but I didn't know where the path led. It might just stop against a briar patch for all I knew. And I couldn't turn back.

There was a flash of lightning; after an interval a low rumble of thunder, then rain began to fall. And I ran. The feet thudded behind me. There was a low-hanging bush and I ducked under it. That's what saved my life. Because the blow only grazed my head and landed with full force on my collarbone. I went out like a blown candle.

12

Someone was shouting. As I moved my head I winced and put up my hand gropingly. There was a bandage on my forehead. I opened my eyes and saw Dr. Ames beside my bed.

"What happened to me?" I asked in surprise. "And who is making all that noise?"

"Your friend Maitland." The doctor managed a smile, which was pretty good going for a man in his late forties who had answered three night calls and was carrying his usual burden. "He's raising hell with the police." As Joe's voice went on shouting, using some of the most blood-curdling threats I'd ever heard, the doctor began to chuckle. "Either," he said, "he'll get you round-the-clock guards or this telephone will be taken out and he'll be put under hatches."

"Not Joe," I said and laughed exultantly.

"O the blood more stirs
To rouse a lion than to start a hare."

"My God!" Mrs. Oliphant ejaculated from her own room. "Shakespeare! What did you see in the man, Sue?"

"His money!" I called back.

Dr. Ames picked up his bag. "I can get you a nurse though you don't need her. Anyhow, Maitland would probably insist on arming her with a shotgun and a club. But you'll be up and prancing around tomorrow. Only please don't prance until you know where you are going. If not for your sake, for mine."

"What happened to me?"

"You knocked yourself out against a tree stump. Got a cut on your forehead. Only one stitch so don't try to make it important; and you nearly broke a collarbone. Got a nasty knock there. Uncomfortable, but you'll live. Now if you and Mrs. Oliphant will just look where you are going — and why you had to be tearing along that path in the woods —"

"Someone was tearing after me. That's why. I have a strong sense of self-preservation, whatever you may think, Dr. Ames. I ran because up to now there have been three murders and one miss. The miss was Mrs. Oliphant who was thrown down the stairs in mistake for Paula. And there's a murderer in the house next door. I don't know which one, but the murderer was right behind me on that path."

Dr. Ames sat down again and cut off any further comment by sticking a thermometer in my mouth. When he removed it I said stormily, "I am not feverish, I am not deliri-

153

ous. Barry was murdered and so was Paula and so was Luella."

"But your sister —"

"She didn't kill herself. Ask Joe. Ask Mrs. Oliphant. Ask the police."

The doctor surveyed me. "There is a certain stimulation about your conversation, Miss Wales."

There was a tap on the door, as light, as cautious as a mouse peeking out of its hole for a cat.

"Come in," the doctor said.

Joe opened the door a crack. "How bad is it, doctor? How . . ." His voice was just above a whisper.

"Come in," the doctor called irritably. Joe stood inside, looking at the bandage on my forehead.

"Is she . . . ?" he croaked.

"She's a damned nuisance," Dr. Ames told him. "If she tries to make any appeal to your sympathy she is faking."

"Dr. Ames," I said as he started out, "you've known the Hamiltons a long time. What did you honestly think of Blanche's performance at the hospital this morning?"

"As a physician —"

"As a man who has had to cope with three violent deaths and two accidents this is no time to be coy."

Mrs. Oliphant called, "That's the stuff to give the troops! Dick, you can trust her. She

154

has a good head; she just sounds silly."

It was a dubious tribute but at least it worked. "I know very little about Mrs. Thomas Hamilton. Theoretically, I see no less reason why aging women can't buy young lovers than aging men, and heaven knows it doesn't seem to hurt the men, either socially or in — to use a revolting phrase — their public image. But I simply don't like that woman. This morning I couldn't figure out whether she was abysmally stupid or really malignant. The whole family knows that John Hamilton's heart is bad. With luck he could go on for years. With a sudden shock he could go out in a minute. But that anyone would cold-bloodedly try to bring about a heart attack in a harmless old man —"

"What caused his attack last night?" I asked.

"Obviously the discovery of Miss Matthews' murder."

"Why? I mean why obviously? Mr. Hamilton was devoted to Barry and completely dependent on him but he came through the shock of his death without a heart attack. He was fond of Paula but he didn't succumb when she was drowned the same day. But Luella — he didn't even like the girl much. He thought she was a bore and a nuisance. He told me so."

"But three violent deaths —"

"No, there's something else. There has to be. Something he knows or guesses about Luella's death. He seems absentminded and unobservant, but he just runs away from things. Actually he observes a lot. And if he really knows something, I think we ought to make sure the murderer can't get at him."

The doctor looked at me, went out heavily, and I heard him in Mrs. Oliphant's room, using her telephone. "I want a private room and round-the-clock nurses for John Hamilton. No visitors are to be admitted under any pretext."

He put down the telephone. "Though who is going to pay for this I don't know, at least until Hamilton's estate is settled. And even then the family can say they didn't order it."

"I'll take care of it," Joe called. He approached the bed as though he were walking on eggs and touched my cheek with a finger tip. Apparently he thought I was labeled: *Fragile, Handle with Care.* "What's all this about Blanche and Mr. Hamilton?"

I told him about my visit to the hospital and my second encounter with Blanche when I went to the Hamilton house to go through Paula's belongings.

The reason I had left the house by the back way and eventually followed the path into the woods was that I hadn't wanted to pass the living room where Ruth and Warren were having a terrific quarrel. Apparently,

156

from what I could gather, she wanted to know why he hadn't answered his telephone when she had called him about Luella. Where had he been? Warren said he had been home all night but he was catching up on arrears of work so he hadn't answered the phone. As a rule, summer calls that late at night were drunken pranks. Of course, he had heard the phone ring.

Dr. Ames, who had been with Mrs. Oliphant, came to the door of my room. "Then our friend King is lying. Just as I was starting for the Hamilton house in response to Miss Wales's call, King was returning home and parking his car. He lives across the street from me and I saw him distinctly."

When the doctor had gone, Joe and I sat staring at each other. Warren King? The tame lawyer?

"Why?" I asked at last blankly. "Ruth was really hysterical this afternoon, and you remember how she was last night. Stunned. Do you suppose it was because Warren wasn't at home, because she was afraid he had no alibi for Luella's murder?"

"The only thing I can see really frightening her," Joe said, "would be to have her one chance of marriage slip through her fingers. That's the hell of a big stake for a woman like Ruth. What I can't see is Warren King chasing you through the woods. When I found you there, with blood on your face, I could have ripped all the Hamiltons apart."

"You found me?"

"I found you. Mrs. Oliphant said you'd gone over to the Hamilton house, and I didn't like it. Walking into the lion's den. And you'd been there nearly two hours. I went over and Blanche told me you had left some time before. So I searched that damned house from top to bottom."

"Joe, you didn't!"

"I did. Warren King tried to stop me. I'd have beaten him to a pulp if Webb hadn't stepped in." He looked regretful. "So then I — took a look at the swimming pool and the guesthouse. And there was nothing left but that little path and there you were, bleeding," he said with his usual delicacy of expression, "like a stuck pig. When I was carrying you over here I saw Warren watching. He didn't offer to help."

"I don't think it was Warren who hit me. I think it was Tommy."

"What!"

So I told him about Tommy barging in when Dexter was telling me he couldn't figure out why Luella was killed instead of Blanche, and Tommy had really hit the roof. He had called me Little Miss Fixit and said to keep my nose out of what didn't concern me, and he had scared hell out of me.

"What was all this in aid of?"

"Well, you remember the police looked for

158

the luggage he had said Blanche was packing and he knew one of us must have tipped them off. Oh, and Blanche said it wasn't healthy to make any claims and I said not with a murderer in the house. And I told Tommy before he jumped on me he'd better keep his wife from trying to give his father a heart attack."

Joe groaned. "I can see that the only way to keep you safe is to get a leash. Instead of an engagement ring I'll buy you a dog collar."

"Speaking of collars. . . ." I put my hand to my collarbone, trying to look fragile and apathetic. I doubt if I succeeded but at least I got results. Joe remembered that we were supposed to be engaged and he discovered that, properly handled, I wouldn't break.

II

"And what," I asked as severely as I could, after what had proved to be a highly satisfactory indication of things to come, "were you doing while I was being clonked on the head?"

"When you clonked yourself on the head," Joe corrected me, "by diving head-on into a tree stump. But when I get my hands on the guy who hurt you —"

159

"Don't evade the question. Where were you all day?"

He had been with the police. By now they were pretty well sold on the idea that the Hamilton murders had no political origin, that they were the work of an insider. And the starting point, the heart of the matter, was the first murder, that of Barry Hamilton. So it meant beginning all over and taking a fresh look.

"Wait," Mrs. Oliphant wailed, "I'm missing things. I held out as long as it was tactful but I can't stand this suspense any longer. For heaven's sake, talk louder."

Joe laughed and went in to prop pillows on her chaise longue and came back to deposit me there with loving care. Mrs. Oliphant took a long look at me and sniffed. "His money, indeed!" she said with what was a ladylike snort. "If you expect me to believe that, stop licking the cream off your whiskers."

One thing, Joe said, was pretty clear. Barry's murder hadn't been carefully planned in advance. It had been a spur-of-the-moment business and fantastically risky. He had been killed in broad daylight in a house filled with people. The chances of being caught in the act were hair-raising. Which meant either that he was killed in a moment of senseless rage or that, for some unknown reason, he had to be killed at that particular time.

The senseless rage and the lack of premeditation had to be ruled out because of the fact that the murderer had brought a piece of lead pipe with him. That left a motive so overwhelming that the murderer was willing to take, or was forced to take, tremendous chances.

Of course, when Luella discovered that the Masters script was gone, everyone jumped to the conclusion that Barry had been killed to prevent publication of the book.

"Well, look at it," Joe said. "Here was an apparently united family, living in loving harmony and all dependent to some extent on the breadwinner. There wasn't a scrap of suspicion against any of them. Then, when Paula died, no one whispered a word about her quarrel with Barry so she was supposed to have killed herself for grief while, and I quote, of unsound mind."

I stirred and made a faint sound and Joe came to sit on the floor beside my chair, wiry hair standing on end, his face intent, his usually kind mouth harder than I had ever guessed it could be.

"So then we arrive on the scene to throw a monkey wrench into the works. Not just because Sue refused to let King wangle her out of the Hamilton money until she knew the score but because she refused to believe that Paula had committed suicide. Then Mrs. Oliphant told us that Paula had left her hus-

161

band, that all was not sweetness and light in the Hamilton ménage, and that someone had pushed her down the stairs in an attempt to kill Paula."

What had appeared to be a couple of highly successful operations were now in the spotlight and under scrutiny. The killer had to go back to the drawing board.

All day Joe had been working with the police, trying to figure what alibis could be established for the time of Barry's murder. Mrs. Hamilton was in her room taking a nap. Mr. Hamilton was in the dining room polishing a loving cup he had won at the age of eighteen for some school activity. "Keeping the memories bright," he said. Tommy was practicing short shots on the lawn. Ruth was gathering wild flowers in the woods, incidentally the only time she had ever been known to do so. There wasn't a scrap of corroboration for one of these alibis.

Nor was there, it turned out, for Warren King, who claimed to have been in his office all day, but could not substantiate the claim because his clerk had been on vacation, he had interviewed no clients, and he had had no telephone calls memorable enough for anyone to remember.

In fact, the only two of the people most clearly involved had alibis. Dexter Webb had been in his New York office and later had taken an author out for cocktails and dinner.

The other alibi was a humdinger. That was Blanche Hamilton's. Mrs. Oliphant had seen her outside Barry's study shortly before the murder was discovered. When she was looked for, she was in her room, apparently fast asleep.

"Right now, the police are doing everything they can to find out all there is to know about Blanche, to run down a motive. Certainly she's not a woman to kill just for the hell of it. Unfortunately we aren't getting much co-operation from Egypt these days and we're not likely to, particularly if some government official was bribed to secure Blanche's release. But copies of that snapshot are being tried on for size here and there."

Something in Joe's voice made me say, "But you don't really believe it was Blanche."

"What gets me is that she and Tommy have been living here for over a year. Then why all of a sudden would she flare up? Oh, you don't believe it's Blanche either."

"I certainly don't think she chased me through the woods. She is overweight and tightly corseted and not athletic. But Tommy, Blanche and Tommy working together — and," I went on more quickly, "if Mr. Hamilton saw something or guessed — after all, Tommy is his son. It would be a terrible thing. More terrible than death."

163

III

To my disgust Dr. Ames had said I was not to have cocktails that night so, being reasonable, I compromised by having just a small one. While Mrs. Oliphant and Joe were heartlessly enjoying a second, I had a tray in my room. What with one thing and another I was half asleep when Carry came to pick up my tray and ask whether I could see a visitor.

"Who is it?"

"Miss Hamilton. She said she wouldn't stay long."

When Ruth came into the room she looked a lot worse than I felt. Her eyes were red and puffy. She was dead white. She sagged as though the vitality had run out of her.

"Come in."

"I just heard about your accident. What on earth happened?"

As Joe had threatened to beat the stuffing out of me if I did any more careless talking I said, "I was running through the woods and stumbled and knocked myself out on a tree stump. No damage except a cut on my forehead and a sore collarbone."

"Oh."

"Do sit down." I hoped she would make it before she fell down. "That's fresh water on the table."

By holding the glass with both hands she

164

managed a few sips. She recovered fast and even managed a faint laugh. "What on earth made you run through the woods?"

"It was beginning to rain and there was lightning. I'm afraid of electric storms."

"Oh." She spoke more quietly this time. "So many terrible things have been happening that I was afraid — that is, I didn't want anything to happen to you."

"Neither do I."

Her eyes met mine, shifted away. "You be very careful from now on."

"I'll do that."

Ruth worried a handkerchief. "Blanche says you came over to look through Paula's belongings."

"Yes, I left the clothes there. Perhaps someone can make use of them."

"The Good Will box. That's what we usually do. You know, Paula left behind everything Barry had given her when she moved over here."

"Yes, she would."

Ruth got up. She wanted to go as much as I wanted her to go but she didn't know how. "Well, I must get back. Mother has been too upset to take charge and I'll have to make the arrangements and there will be an inquest, of course."

"How is your father?"

"Dr. Ames says no visitors. Both Tommy and I have tried all afternoon to see him."

165

"I suppose rest is the best thing for a heart case."

"I suppose so." Ruth made another abortive attempt to leave. "Oh, I forgot. Blanche wanted me to ask whether, when you were going through Paula's things, you happened to find a bottle of perfume, black with a crystal stopper. It's something special she has made for her in Europe. She can't find it."

"I didn't," I said levelly, "look in Blanche's room for Paula's belongings."

"Well, of course not. She just thought —"

After all, I wasn't sleepy. Ruth had come to find out what happened to me. Whether she believed me or not I couldn't tell, but she had given me a warning to be careful.

Had Blanche realized belatedly that her perfume might betray her and suggested that someone had taken it? Had someone else carried the bottle and sprayed the room so that, if I realized it had been searched, I would blame Blanche? But in that case the person who had used that spray must have brought back some traces of the powerful, cloying, clinging stuff.

I eased my position and went back over that ugly and frightening experience in the woods. Silly or not, I reached out to switch on the reading lamp beside the bed.

166

13

Joe had gone again by the time I woke up in the morning. At Mrs. Oliphant's suggestion I had my tray in her room, my chair drawn close to the window so that I could report on developments next door.

"Joe didn't even leave a message for me," I complained.

"I can't figure why he isn't sleepwalking," Mrs. Oliphant said. "I was so uncomfortable with this beastly cast that I couldn't rest and I think the man must have looked into your room about every half hour to make sure you were still alive. How long do you think you can keep him in this state of infatuation?"

"I don't know, but it's wonderful while it lasts."

She smiled. "This helps balance some of that horror next door. I haven't even listened to the news."

I hadn't either. I had slept soundly and as the doctor had foretold, I felt fine this morning and hungry as a wolf.

Bathing had been more uncomfortable than I had expected, and I had some trouble in getting into my clothes and finally had to ask

167

Carry to zip me up.

Dr. Ames, she said, was with Mrs. Oliphant and he would see me in a few minutes. When he did he replaced the bandage with a small dressing and a Bandaid.

"I've promised Mrs. Oliphant to replace that heavy cast with a lighter one. She'll be much more comfortable." He straightened up. "Well, both my patients seem to be on the mend." He didn't sound particularly cheerful over our recovery. "Do you people check the locks at night?" he asked unexpectedly. "Oh, I forgot, Maitland is staying here. That man is an army in himself."

"Dick, come back here," Mrs. Oliphant called. "Something has happened. I can tell by your voice."

We both went into her room. "John Hamilton died last night," he said somberly.

"Oh, no! Those poor people. As though they were being wiped out one at a time. It's unspeakable."

"It's all of that. And this was partly my own fault. I overlooked —"

"Your fault, Dick? Don't be absurd. You did all you could for the man."

"Except that I forgot there was a telephone in that private room."

"Someone called him," I said at last in a small shaken voice.

"Someone called him. By sheer chance the operator overheard the conversation. The caller

168

said, 'There will be another death.' That was all. And Hamilton's heart stopped."

"So that was murder too," Mrs. Oliphant said.

"That was murder too. I've just come from the Hamilton house. I didn't tell Mrs. Hamilton the reason for her husband's heart failure. She has collapsed completely. Ruth is trying to cope but she acts like an automaton. I think she had absorbed about as much punishment as she can take."

When Dr. Ames had gone I went back to sit with Mrs. Oliphant. I didn't want to be alone. We didn't talk much. We just sat staring at nothing and wondering which one — which one.

Late in the morning Dexter Webb came to say he'd heard about my accident from Ruth and to ask how I was. With Mrs. Oliphant's permission I had him come up to her room. After greeting us he dropped into a chair, his head resting against a cushion.

As he fumbled in his pocket and then dropped his hand, Mrs. Oliphant said, "Go ahead and smoke. It won't bother me at all."

"Thanks." He gave her his engaging smile. "You are a very observant woman."

Her eyes twinkled. "That isn't a quality that has endeared me to the Hamiltons." Then she sobered. "Poor things. Poor poor things."

"It's just plain hell. I think everyone in the

169

place has had to be put under sedation except Tommy and this morning he looks as though he'd be next. His father's death seems to have shocked him greatly though he must have known how serious the old boy's condition was and that he might go at any time."

"Especially if he were given a slight push," I said.

"Push! But he wasn't —"

"Someone called him last night and said there would be another death. That's what killed him."

Dexter put down the pipe he had started to fill and stared at me. "Sue, what in God's name are you saying?"

"Ask Dr. Ames. The telephone operator at the hospital overheard the call."

"But no one would do a thing like that."

"Blanche would. She tried yesterday morning when I was visiting Mr. Hamilton."

"But, my dear, why on earth should Blanche do a thing like that? She's not an attractive person but that doesn't make her a criminal."

"Well, something does. She was arrested in Egypt for the murder of a former husband and bought her way out. And she was right outside Barry's study just about the time he was killed, though she appeared to be sound asleep a few minutes later. And she was right on the spot when Luella was killed. And

170

someone using her perfume searched my bedroom here and —"

Dexter leaned back in his chair. "Good God!" he said limply. "Ever since the thing was brought home to us I've been thinking until I've gone nearly crazy. It seemed to me that everyone could be eliminated except Warren. It's true that Barry and Tommy never hit it off and there was a good deal of tension between them during the last months, but Tommy wouldn't have killed his own brother. So that left Warren, though what conceivable motive he had I couldn't figure. But I never thought of a woman."

He broke off. "Look here, both of you have had more than enough of the Hamilton tragedies. How about you, Sue? Ruth says you fell over a tree stump and knocked yourself out yesterday. She was pretty upset about it."

"I didn't want to tell Ruth what happened. Someone was chasing me."

"You saw someone chasing you?" Dexter was incredulous.

"No, I didn't see who it was, but I heard him behind me, and you know how Tommy acted when I was talking to you in Barry's study. He was just vicious."

"How bad is it?" Dexter's lips tightened. "I guess I've got so accustomed to regarding him as a harmless playboy that I didn't take him seriously."

171

"It's not bad at all. A painful collarbone and a small cut on my forehead. I'm responsible for that one myself but it saved my life."

"I can't figure it out. Not Tommy. Ruth said that Warren saw Maitland carrying you across the lawn. If anyone, I'd have thought — well —" He got up, a man so tired he could barely stand. For a moment he took my hand, looking down soberly at me. He was a very tall man. "You be careful. Get Maitland to look after you."

"He will." I was confident about that.

Something in my expression made Dexter laugh. "That's fine." He smiled at Mrs. Oliphant and left, going back to the hell next door.

When he had gone Mrs. Oliphant sighed. "What a pity Paula didn't marry that man. But I can tell you right now, young woman, when Joe Maitland hears about the way you have been carrying on, especially after he warned you —"

"What has she done now?" Joe asked from the doorway.

Mrs. Oliphant told him what I had said to Dexter. He was not amused. "Not only a leash and a dog collar," he said grimly, "but a muzzle. You haven't the sense of a rabbit, Sue."

"Well," I repeated rather heatedly, "there's no secret about the way Mr. Hamilton died.

172

Dr. Ames told us himself."

"What! Hamilton is dead?"

When I had told him about the telephone call that had resulted in John Hamilton's fatal heart attack Joe said, "That settles it. Either I lock you up myself, or I have you taken into protective custody, or I march you back to Pennsylvania."

"The police probably won't let us go until after the inquest into Luella's death."

"I'd better call them about Hamilton. They don't know about that. I've just come from there."

That morning he and Lieutenant Graby had been trying to see whether anyone could be eliminated for Paula's murder. But with the house in a state of confusion, police milling around, it was impossible except in the case of Mrs. Hamilton who had collapsed when she learned of Barry's death. Blanche was supposedly drugged with a heavy dose of sleeping pills. Ruth had not returned to the house for more than an hour. Gathering wild flowers, she had said.

"Did she have any?" I asked.

Joe shrugged. He had no idea. "The more we talked about it, the more incredible it seemed that anyone would dare — with police in the house — to attack Paula."

"I've thought and thought. She came running when Mrs. Oliphant was hurt and called Dr. Ames. He came here from the Hamilton

173

house where he had seen Barry's body. He was the one who told Paula what had happened. And she helped him with the cast. She must have guessed, when she saw the robe Mrs. Oliphant was wearing, what had happened. Joe, when I think of what must have been happening to her inside I can't bear it! Because, whatever had gone wrong the day before she had been madly in love with Barry. That didn't just stop overnight. And now to know she was threatened. Oh, God! Not Paula."

"Steady there, darling." As usual Joe's voice was like having strong arms around me, comforting me.

"I'm all right. I'm just trying to understand. Paula must have been pretty sure what had happened. She left a message for me."

"But why wouldn't she have told Mrs. Oliphant or Dr. Ames?"

"I was in shock," Mrs. Oliphant said. "I don't suppose I'd have been much help."

"Anyhow, I think Paula had to be sure. She couldn't call me from here because the telephone is in Mrs. Oliphant's room. I think she went back, found the house full of police, and tried to use the extension phone on the terrace. And the murderer stopped her and put her in the pool."

"It could have happened that way," Joe admitted. "And there's one thing I'm pretty sure of. Whether Blanche killed him or not,

174

I'd be willing to swear that she saw Barry's body and then got out from under as fast as she could by taking the sleeping pills. With her past record she simply couldn't afford being involved in another crime. Egypt is a long way off and we have few friends there, but, with publicity brought to bear, her story would be bound to come out. Old newspaper accounts. Something."

"There's one thing I'm pretty sure of too," I said. "Somewhere in Barry's files there will be notes about the book Luella mentioned, the one Barry was going to write if someone wasn't reasonable. Luella was threatening someone. I suppose Dexter will let us know what he finds."

"It strikes me that the files should have been examined by the police in the first place."

"Well, Dexter won't cover up anything."

What had the police stymied was the third murder. There should have been traffic signals to keep people from running into each other in the study: Luella, Ruth, Blanche, and the murderer. What had brought Luella there at that time of night?

"Considering the way she shot off her mouth at dinner, I think she was probably and belatedly guarding the files. She must have realized someone would want to know what Barry had been up to."

"And there is still the Masters script," Mrs.

175

Oliphant said. "We've rather lost sight of that. I wonder if Barry really did dig up anything juicy."

"I can tell you one thing," I said, "if there was anything dishonest in that book, Paula would have dropped it flat."

"And dropped Barry too?"

"I think so. Yes. There doesn't seem to have been any other reason for the sudden breakup of the marriage. Barry had just finished the book. He must have given it to her to read. One day everything was honeymoon. The next day it was over. Paula could never have compromised on a thing as terribly important as a book that would not only ruin a man's career but that might even change the national political picture. Only —"

"What is it?"

"Barry was vain and, in my opinion, unscrupulous; he could be cruel, at least in his books. But his father told me he adored Paula, that he would have done anything for her. So if he and Paula quarreled about the book, what happened?"

"We'll never know unless we can find the missing script."

The maid brought sherry, and Joe led the talk to vintage wines and famous vineyards and then anchored it firmly in Spain. For a little while we managed to put aside the horror of the murders.

After lunch Joe and I sat out on the lawn

176

chairs under a big umbrella and talked lazily. We must see Dexter and find out what he was learning about the files. But the afternoon was hot and there was shade where we were. We just sat, holding hands, and now and then making some tentative plan for the future. I hadn't realized that happiness could be so quiet, that it needed no words; that deep contentment is better than gaiety.

Even with the unleashed violence next door in the house from which four people had gone to their deaths, it was possible to imagine a good future. Once Joe switched on a little transistor radio and then switched it off quickly but not in time. A commentator was suggesting with a laugh that the Hamilton house be declared a disaster area. I hoped he would lose his job for that piece of misplaced humor.

There wasn't a sound but the faint sibilant rustling of leaves and the sleepy chirping of a bird. Then Blanche came around the side of the house like a whirlwind. I wouldn't have believed so heavy a woman could move so fast. She was beside us before Joe could struggle out of his chair. She was in the grip of such rage that she was completely out of control. With an impatient gesture she refused the chair Joe offered her, a gesture that set the diamonds on her hand to flashing in the sun. She ignored me, pouring out all her fury at Joe.

"You'd better watch this kid and stop her mouth for her or I'll do it myself. We've had enough trouble over there without your girl butting in. The police have been hammering at me all morning, trying to prove I killed them. Trying to mess around and dig up something out of my past. Trying to find a motive."

She laughed. "If people would use their heads and their eyes they wouldn't need to look far for motives. Barry quarreled with everyone. He was more and more irritable as he got toward the end of his book, on edge and disagreeable. Warren had a big quarrel with him. I gather that Barry had our lawyer over a barrel. Ruth is so much in love with Warren, or she regards him as Custer's Last Stand, that she hated Barry for what he was doing, scaring off her boy friend. She raised hell with him about it. Now you are trying to prove I called his father and scared him into a heart attack. Tommy's in a state. Lay off. Do you hear me?"

"They can probably hear you in Stockford," Joe said.

"What they are going to hear — everyone in Connecticut so far as I am concerned — is that Luella actually heard Paula kill Barry."

"And who," Joe asked, "killed Luella?"

"Dexter Webb," Blanche said promptly. "He was in love with Paula. And Sue's saintly sister was in love with him."

178

"Oh, don't be silly," I said.

"Yeah? Then why did Paula and Barry have an ugly quarrel about Dexter the day she moved out? I heard them. Not that they were talking so loud but they were so — queer —"

"You eavesdropped," Joe said.

"Okay, so I eavesdropped. And that quarrel they had really blew the roof off. Paula was preparing to run away with Dexter."

Blanche came to a full stop, looked from one of us to the other, and then turned and went back toward the Hamilton house.

After a long time, I said, "I don't believe it."

14

Next morning brought the inquest into Luella Matthews' murder. The little courthouse was jammed and there were mobs in the street outside. The Hamilton murders had become big enough news to push even the war off the right side of the newspapers. Reporters, cameramen, summer visitors, natives, all pushed and shoved and tried to get into the small building. I went with Joe, hanging on to his arm so we would not be separated in the crowd.

Never having attended an inquest I expected some dramatic disclosures. So apparently did those mobs of people. But the procedure had been carefully worked out in advance. My part consisted merely in saying that I heard the screams and that I had called the police for the Hamiltons. It was obvious that the police did not want any new information released at the moment. About all that was established was that Luella Matthews had been strangled by a person or persons unknown. The jury added a rider, expressing their sympathy for the grief-stricken Hamiltons.

There was only one awkward question. One of the jurors asked whether Eliot Masters and/or his party could be involved. He was frowned down. No one asked why Ruth was still dressed long after the family had gone to bed. No one asked what Blanche was doing in the study when the body was discovered. The inquest adjourned fast. People drifted away reluctantly, feeling let down as they do at a prize fight when no one is knocked out.

We drove back in that awful heap of Joe's to report to Mrs. Oliphant and then went out to meet Lieutenant Graby. This was my idea. When I had taken that path through the woods, it had occurred to me that the deep carpet of autumn leaves would make an excellent hiding place for the missing Masters script. After all, no one had been allowed to leave the Hamilton house after the murder. It must have been hidden somewhere close at hand.

Joe had accepted the idea more enthusiastically than he did most of mine and he had reported it to the lieutenant. This was why the lieutenant allowed me to be included in the search, over Joe's protests. There were more people than I had expected. The group consisted of Lieutenant Graby, Sergeant Knight, a trooper named Wellcome, and a young man who looked vaguely familiar but whom I could not place. Graby ordered him to leave, and Joe had to do some fast talking

181

to get him included.

"Who is he?" I asked as we started across the lawn toward the Hamilton house.

"A New York reporter, fellow named Fischer. We've got a sort of deal. If he keeps you out of the paper I'll give him an exclusive story."

"What kind of story?"

"Something will turn up." Joe had been unusually silent ever since he had gone over to the Hamilton house early that morning to extend sympathy and offer help if help was needed. Mrs. Hamilton, he was told, had collapsed completely when she heard of her husband's death. Ruth was now planning a double funeral for Luella and her father, the second double funeral in ten days. She looked dazed. The Tommy Hamiltons were in their room. Tommy, Ruth said, had been sick most of the night because of a nervous stomach. The death of his father had been a shock to him. There was no sign of Warren King, who might be expected to offer a helping hand at this time. It was Dexter who had talked to Joe. Dr. Ames was sending someone to stay with Mrs. Hamilton while the others attended the inquest. There was nothing anyone could do.

As our small party approached the guesthouse, heading for the path through the woods, Dexter came out.

"How are you feeling, Sue?"

"Fine."

182

"What's going on?"

"We're going to look for the missing Masters script. It was my idea."

Dexter smiled at Joe who was never more than a foot from me. "You've got yourself a smart girl."

"I'm a smart guy," Joe told him.

"Can you use me? Ruth doesn't want me underfoot in the house."

"Come along. I expected King would be on hand to help Ruth."

"That affair blew up yesterday."

"I must say he picked a hell of a time to add to the girl's troubles," Joe commented.

"Maybe he couldn't help it. I didn't catch what it was all about, and it wasn't any of my business anyhow, but I gathered there had been some kind of trouble between Barry and King, and Ruth was worrying it like a dog with a bone. Everyone has been on edge, naturally. Perhaps they'll patch things up later."

Lieutenant Graby spread us out, each with a long stick, and we moved slowly, prodding every blanket of leaves. It was slow work and my collarbone began to be uncomfortable from stooping, so I left the job to the others and walked beside Joe. Once in a clearing we saw a fox, the sun bright on its red coat, and then it was gone. There were squirrels and chipmunks. I kept my eyes on the path, hoping there were no snakes. And I kept a

183

sharp lookout for poison ivy, the curse of Connecticut.

Now and then there were false alarms as someone's stick struck a stone or a buried log under the leaves. It was the reporter, Fischer, a slight young man with a prematurely balding head, myopic eyes behind thick glasses, and a nice ugly face, who found the cache.

The leaves had been piled over the package, which had been wrapped in heavy layers of plastic to protect it from the weather and the damp ground. The reporter was a trifle resentful when Graby shoved him aside unceremoniously and had his own men brush off the leaves and haul up the package.

At Dexter's suggestion the package was placed on the long worktable in the guesthouse. For the first time I saw men testing for fingerprints. There were none either on the plastic cover or on the script itself.

We all crowded around, looking over Dexter's shoulder, as he looked at the script. It was entitled, *Strange Company, A Study in Ambition.*

"We'll have to take this with us," Graby said.

Somewhat to my surprise Dexter made no protest though I should have thought he could not wait to get his hands on the book.

Joe said, "What's wrong, Sue? Smell a skunk?"

"I smell Blanche."

The perfume was not as strong as it had been in my room, just the faintest trace, but it was unmistakable.

"She's been in here." With Dexter's rather amused permission, I began to search. I looked in the bathroom, in the small kitchenette, in the clothes closet, feeling my face growing hotter with embarrassment but ignoring the grins on the faces of the police. Then I tried to look under the beds and gave up. It hurt to bend over.

Joe, laughing, looked under one bed and then under the other. He straightened up, an odd look on his face, pulled the bed back from the wall, bent over and drew out a necklace, a long jangling piece of junk jewelry.

"What's this?"

The amusement faded from Dexter's face. "That was Luella's. Someone seems to have been having fun and games in here." He frowned at me. "Are you sure about that perfume?"

I nodded emphatically.

"But what that's supposed to prove . . ."

Graby looked at him thoughtfully and I knew what must be coming. Joe had insisted on reporting everything that had been said to us during Blanche's outburst.

"By the way, Mr. Webb, according to Mrs. Thomas Hamilton, the marriage between Mr.

185

and Mrs. Barry Hamilton had broken up because of you. She claims to have overheard their quarrel."

Dexter looked up at him in blank astonishment. "That," he said steadily, "is without a scrap of foundation. I'll admit I was in love with Mrs. Hamilton practically at first sight but I never had a chance. To the best of my knowledge her marriage to Barry was one of mutual devotion. Whatever caused its breakup, if there was a breakup, had nothing to do with me. If you had known her," his voice was suddenly out of control, as suddenly steady again, "you would have known she was incapable of a shoddy action. Her character was as lovely as her face."

"Okay," the lieutenant said quietly. "But it's as well to check." He looked around for his two men and started out, the script under his arm. "You'll keep us informed of anything you find in Hamilton's files, won't you? You are probably the only person who would be able to evaluate the stuff there."

"Glad to."

"I'll leave it to you then."

When the police had gone Dexter took us up to the house and through the terrace door to the study. While he sat at the big desk, Joe and young Fischer and I pulled up chairs, waiting expectantly.

The desk was heaped with the material from the files, which had been carefully

186

sorted. There were sheaves of reviews from a clipping bureau, volumes of fan mail, two drafts of every one of the books he had done, almost as much in the way of preliminary notes, interviews, and background material.

Whatever Barry had been he had certainly kept a weather eye on posterity. Even his notes were typed on heavy linen paper designed to withstand the ravages of the ages. Each script was bound in blue leather, with the title stamped in gold on the spine.

Joe sat watching Dexter thoughtfully. "You are up to something, my friend. When you let that Masters script go without a protest —"

Dexter grinned. "That was the first thing I found in the files."

"The carbon copy?"

Dexter nodded.

"Why the hell didn't you tell Graby?"

"I'm a publisher, Maitland. And where that book is concerned, time is of the essence. It's been more publicized in advance than anything since the Manchester book. I sent it registered mail to the office yesterday morning."

"Well?"

"Well what?"

"What is in it?"

"I don't know. I don't want to lose another day in reading it. Barry was an old pro, you

187

know. It's safe to let the copy editor handle it and start it through the presses. If any changes have to be made we'll wait for galley proofs."

"You were very sure of Hamilton, weren't you?"

"I've published him for ten years. I ought to be."

It was young Fischer who asked, "Have you unearthed anything from Hamilton's files that might provide a clue to his murder?"

Dexter's fingers did a drumbeat on the desk. "That's really why I wanted you to come here, have a talk. I'm not sure just what the hell I've found, whether it has any connection with the murders or not —"

"I can't stand this suspense," Fischer said.

"There were two unexpected items," Dexter said slowly. He took a thin folder and opened it. "Barry's next book was to be called *Malice Domestic*. It was to be a study of family murders beginning with Greek drama and ending," he paused a moment as though for emphasis, "in Egypt four years ago."

"So that's it!" I said. "That's why Blanche was so upset. That's what Luella meant — you remember she said he was going to do a book if someone wasn't reasonable? Do you think he threatened her?"

Dexter gave me his wry smile. "Now, look here, Sue, I'm showing you the evidence. I don't know what it means, how much bearing it has on the murders. But I thought I'd get the opinions of all of you before turning it over to the police. The Hamiltons have about had it."

"Turn it over," Joe said promptly.

Fischer eyed the folder wistfully, obviously thinking what a lovely scoop it would make, but he nodded agreement with Joe.

"All right," Dexter said. "I'll turn this over to Graby. But I hope to God he'll hold off any action until after that double funeral. Mrs. Hamilton is still under sedation."

"Did you find anything else?" I asked.

"The damnedest thing." Dexter turned over files, pulled out a sheet of paper, glanced at it, pushed it across the desk toward us.

"I acknowledge having spent $7,800 of money given me by Barry Hamilton for investment. This day I will put my house on the market and I will agree to repay the money, with interest, on or before January 1, 1968." It was signed "Warren King."

Beneath it Barry Hamilton had written: "It is understood that if Warren King fails to make full repayment on the date given above that I will put the case in the hands of the law and prosecute."

15

While we had cocktails with Mrs. Oliphant we argued the case back and forth. At least we knew now that Barry Hamilton had intended to put Blanche's case in a book. Or at least he had held the threat over her head unless she decided to be "reasonable." What he hoped to gain by it was something else again unless he always operated, as I believed he did, through pure malice.

Luella had made clear at dinner that she knew about the projected book and it seemed likely that Blanche had been trying to look for the notes the night Luella was attacked.

It was probable, too, that Luella's outburst had brought Ruth to the study too, in an attempt to find out whether Barry had left any memorandum about his quarrel with Warren King. That the lawyer was capable of misusing funds placed in his hands did not particularly surprise me. And I could see why he had been so upset about the possibility of my inheriting the Hamilton estate. If it went to the Hamilton family, Ruth would protect him.

"But could a woman have done it, stran-

190

gled Luella, I mean?" I asked.

"Anyone could do it," Joe said. "She was strangled with her own scarf. A quick jerk, a —" He made a graphic gesture.

"Don't!"

"Sorry," he said, but somehow I did not think he was sorry. He had deliberately meant me to get a vivid picture of that ruthless and brutal murder. It wasn't like Joe. Not like him at all.

Mrs. Oliphant sighed, and Joe helped her get into a more comfortable position. "So far as I can make out, anyone with the exception of his parents, of course, would have had a motive for killing Barry. The same applies to Luella. But Paula? But poor harmless old Mr. Hamilton? Why, Joe? Why?"

He made no reply. He was still quiet at dinner, so absorbed in his thoughts that Carry had to remind him that she was waiting to serve him. When we had finished he said, "I'm going out for a while."

"I want to go with you."

He came over to tilt back my head and kiss me, a long deliberate kiss. "My seal, to keep you safe until I get back."

In the long run he agreed to take me with him, not because he really wanted to but because he didn't dare leave me alone.

Something in the way he spoke made me say sharply, "Joe, do you think you know who it is?"

191

"I think so, but I'm damned if I know why."

"When did you find out?"

"I haven't found out. Just bits and pieces that seem to fit together. And then today when we were in Barry's study — Sue, why didn't you tell me about that mirror?"

"I just forgot and I know what you mean. Barry saw his killer."

Joe nodded. He said thoughtfully, "Paula. Oh, don't."

"You don't believe that?" I was furious.

"I think," he said, "that is what Luella thought she heard. That would account for everything else."

"I don't understand." Joe made no answer. I tried again. "Where are we going?"

"I'd like to have a talk with friend King. Where was he when Barry was killed? Where was he when Luella was killed? It's a cinch he wasn't home. He lied about that as Dr. Ames saw him returning home just as he started out in answer to your call."

As the evening had turned cool I got a light coat and Joe helped me into the heap. He had just reached the road when he braked as hard as he could, nearly sending me through the windshield.

"Fasten that seat belt!" he snapped. "I've told you a dozen times."

"I wouldn't need it if this thing drove like a decent car instead of leaping like a kanga-

192

roo," I muttered, while I fastened the seat belt obediently. Then I saw why Joe had stopped. The Chrysler was leaving the Hamilton house. The driver had let it roll down the driveway without starting the motor or switching on lights. Now he did both. Tonight there were no lurking newsmen. Perhaps the disappointment over the inquest had disheartened them, or they believed that the end had come to the Hamilton tragedies.

"It's Dexter! Where on earth is he going, sneaking off like that? It doesn't seem like him."

Joe let the Chrysler get as far ahead as he dared and then, using dimmers, followed to the village. For a moment we thought we had lost the Chrysler and then we saw it parked on the Green. The driver got out and a corner street light touched the brown hair. It wasn't Dexter, it was Ruth Hamilton. Joe turned onto the Green, parked a few slots away, and waited while Ruth went rapidly toward the corner and down the street.

"She's going to Warren's office," I said.

Joe switched off the motor and started after her.

"Wait for me," I called.

"You stay in the car. Oh, hell, I can't trust you alone. Come along, but do as you're told."

There were no lights in Warren's office. Then we saw them go on and the blinds

193

were hastily pulled down. There was only a forty-watt bulb at the top of the stairs. We went up as quietly as we could, Joe turned the knob, and eased the door open.

Ruth was alone in Warren's private office, looking through his desk. When she saw us I thought she was going to faint. There was no fight in her. Joe eased her into a chair and I brought her a paper cup of water. And after while she began to cry, hard racking sobs. When I started to speak, Joe shook his head warningly.

At length the sobs slowed down, except for an occasional hiccup that shook her body. She blew her nose and wiped her eyes.

"What are you doing here?" she asked at last.

"We followed you," Joe said. "We're after the same thing, you know."

"What's that?"

"The truth about this business."

"I just had to know." She seemed too tired to care any more. "Dr. Ames told us how my father died. Someone deliberately caused him a fatal shock. Someone just goes on and on and on. So I had to know. Because it's got to stop. No matter."

"It's got to stop," Joe agreed. "No matter."

Her hands lay open and relaxed on her lap, empty and curiously pathetic, busy hands that had no work to do. She began to talk and Joe motioned for me to keep quiet. She

194

and Warren had known each other since he had moved to Stockford years ago and had become Barry's lawyer and later his man of business. Barry hated bothering with investments and handling money. It confused and bored him. So she and Warren were thrown together a lot.

Most of the story was left unsaid. She was thirty-nine and unmarried. Warren was a bachelor and available. But they just seemed to remain good friends. Sometimes she had wondered whether a girl should know how to give a hint of some kind. She gave me a puzzled look but one in which there was no resentment. Paula had made men love her terribly, even a man like Barry who had never before cared more for someone else than for himself. Of course Paula had been very beautiful. And I seemed to have that knack, whatever it was. Her dull eyes drifted to Joe, drifted away again. I was sick with pain and humiliation for her.

It was her mother, she thought, who had kind of brought things about. Nothing was actually said, but she and Warren had drifted into a kind of understanding. They would be married someday though no plans were made. Or maybe, like Luella, she had just thought so.

Then, shortly before her brother died, he and Warren had had a flaming row. Neither of them had mentioned it to her but she thought Barry disliked the idea of her marrying the lawyer.

"I asked Barry about it and he just laughed. He said they had quarreled but it wasn't about me. If Warren were interested in me he hadn't shown any signs of it. Barry could be — well, unkind."

In any case, Warren had stayed away from the house until Barry was murdered. The dreary voice went on with the dreary story. At once, she said, they began to make plans for their wedding. That, I realized, must have been after I had told him over the telephone that I didn't want Paula's estate.

It wasn't until after Luella was killed and she couldn't reach Warren and the fact emerged that the murders were not the work of a political group that she became frightened. Warren told her he had been working at home that night and she didn't know what to believe.

"Well, he came next morning and I had to know. I was so terribly afraid because of the way Luella had talked about Barry's quarrels, and all like that. And finally Warren said it was ridiculous to believe that he and Barry had quarreled about me. There was no motive. Barry and he had never discussed me at all. In fact, Warren said he was afraid there was some awkward sort of misunderstanding between us and he was engaged to another girl and he had been with her at the time Luella was killed. He had been trying to spare my feelings." She started to laugh, a note of hysteria in her voice.

"Steady." Joe's voice was like a strong hand held to a drowning man.

"I shouldn't have been so surprised. I even know who the girl is. It — that is, I followed Warren there the afternoon Barry was killed, when I was supposed to be in the woods gathering wild flowers. I'd been worrying about that quarrel with Barry and I knew it was Warren's slack season at the office, and he hadn't come to the house, so —"

He had been leaving the office and hadn't noticed her. She had followed him to a small house on the outskirts of the village. Warren had driven around the house and parked at the back as though he didn't want his presence to be noticed. She — after a moment's struggle with the last fragments of her pride, Ruth said she had peeked in the windows. They were going upstairs.

She had blamed herself and blamed Barry because they had not married sooner. After all, a man was a man. It wasn't anything important to him. But now she wasn't sure. Not sure about anything.

"Suppose," Joe said, "we give up all these speculations for a while and consider the evidence." He ran a hand through his unruly hair. "It isn't here, you know. Webb found it in Barry's files." He told her bluntly about

197

the statement the lawyer had signed.

After a long time Ruth said, in a dead voice, "So that's it."

"Do you believe your brother would really have prosecuted?" Joe asked.

Ruth had no doubt at all. "Oh, yes. Barry could be very generous; in fact, he was very generous. But in many ways he was a hard man. He would never have let anyone cheat him."

"At least," Joe tried to break through that sodden despair, "you know now that their quarrel was not about you."

This did not cheer Ruth. "No. I never really mattered at all, did I?"

Joe's round eyes studied her for a moment. "I have a curious idea," he said at last, "that your friend Warren is a chivalrous idiot." He was facing the door and I felt that he was not speaking to her at all. "I suspect that he has been trying to protect you by making clear that you had no motive for quarreling with either Barry or Luella."

"I don't understand."

Now I could see Warren King standing motionless just inside the hall door.

"Well, you had no alibi for Barry's murder and you were right on hand when Luella died, the only member of the family who was still dressed. Luella had pointed out that you had quarreled with Barry. I think King wanted to establish the fact that no suspicion

198

could fall on you because you had no reason for quarreling with either of them. So far as that little difficulty of his with Barry was concerned, he must have known that you would understand how it happened and clear things for him as soon as the estate fell into your hands, as it will probably do, to a large extent, at least."

"Well I — of course —"

"By the way," Joe asked, "just why the hell were you in the study the night Luella was strangled?"

"After she talked so much I knew something was wrong. I wanted to see for myself whether Barry had left any record. And I found Blanche there — and she screamed — and then I saw Luella —"

Warren came slowly into his inner office, his eyes searching Joe's face. But, after all, Joe had written the script for him. All he had to do was to read the lines. He moved awkwardly toward Ruth.

"Mr. Maitland is right. I never believed for a moment that you were guilty but —"

"Oh, Warren!"

We were nearly home before I spoke. "Do you think she believed you?"

"She wants to; that's the important thing." If there is anything that infuriates me it is the average man's conviction that any woman is better off with any man than with no man at all.

I swallowed hard. "Look here, there wasn't a word of truth in that, was there?"

"Well, I doubt very much if Warren ever thought seriously of marrying Ruth until he began to dip his fingers in the till. I suppose he thought she'd be a line of defense if he got caught. He doesn't seem to have known Barry very well. But when Barry was killed and you were prepared to give up the money, he tried to get things sewed up before anything about that signed statement of his came to light. Unfortunately for our tame lawyer he wasn't prepared to give up his sordid little romance so he got caught without an alibi he dared to claim. But now, with the old man gone and Tommy not needing the Hamilton money, Ruth will be well fixed."

"Will she?" I asked gloomily.

16

At seven in the morning there was still dew on the grass and a rabbit nibbled at the edge of the lawn. Somewhere a cardinal uttered its clear repetitive notes. In the distance there was the whirr of an electric lawnmower as someone worked before the heat of the day. Where the sun slanted through the woods the trunks of trees looked almost red. Leaves sparkled as though the world had just been freshly washed.

There was a pot of coffee in the kitchen and I poured a cup and took it out onto the lawn. For once I was ahead of Joe who, apparently, was catching up on sleep.

It was still early when I walked into the village and went once more to the florist. This was the morning of the double funeral, which was being held as privately as possible to escape curious sightseers and reporters. I didn't want to go. I had never seen Paula's grave and I didn't want to see it. She wasn't there, not the lovely Paula I knew; she was alive for me and I wanted to keep her like that, to be able to take out my memories and see them smiling and hopeful and bright.

201

Joe understood how I felt and he had decided to take me to New York for the day. Anyhow, he said, he had to see a man. He had ordered masses of flowers to be sent to the funeral parlor at the top of the Green. The last time I had come to the florist it was to buy roses for Mr. Hamilton. Today I selected pink and white carnations, spicy and sweet, and I insisted on carrying them myself, though the florist assured me they would be delivered to the funeral parlor where the services were to be held. But I wanted my flowers for the living.

The door of the Hamilton house was opened for me by Dexter, looking unexpectedly remote and formal in a dark suit, white shirt and black necktie.

"Good morning, Sue," he said in the hushed voice that accompanies death as though one would awaken those quiet sleepers. "I understand that flowers are being sent straight to the funeral parlor. Would you like me to take care of them for you?"

"Not these," I said firmly. "The carnations are for Mrs. Hamilton."

His tired face lighted up. "How like you! She'll love them."

"What is it?" Ruth asked. She had come out of the living room, fairly dripping with mourning, including black stockings, but her face was alive and glowing. Behind her I saw Warren, looking suitably grave, a black armband around his sleeve.

"Sue brought these carnations for your mother."

Ruth was surprised. "Mother?" Then she was pleased. "Mother would be delighted. Why don't you go up and see her, Sue? I'll put these in water and bring them along. She's getting ready for the service."

"She won't mind having me?"

"Of course," Ruth said warningly, "she doesn't know about that telephone call to Father. She's just in a daze, what with the sedation she's had and one thing and another. Dr. Ames said we shouldn't tell her yet. If she rambles a bit you'll understand. She can't seem to stop talking, though she doesn't make much sense."

I assured her that I would understand. Mrs. Hamilton, half dressed, sat at her dressing table, a hairbrush in her hand, her eyes with an oddly unfocused look.

"Oh, Sue," she said without surprise, rather as though we were continuing a conversation, "I can't seem to remember where Ruth put the dress I wore at the other funerals. I think I spilled something on it. Maybe Ruth sent it to the cleaner. Cleaners are so unreliable these days, aren't they?"

In her closet I found a black dress still in the plastic bag in which it had come from the cleaner. "Is this the one you want?"

"Thank you, my dear. How very kind of

you. Usually Ruth would be helping me but she has her hands full and I don't like to bother her. Lately she has been so unhappy, poor thing. Any woman ought to be able to manage to marry if she goes about it right, don't you think? But Ruth just drifted along. If I hadn't finally taken a hand and just plain asked Warren where they were planning to live after they were married, I don't think he'd have done anything about it. Ruth doesn't know how to take care of herself, if you know what I mean, and so terribly angry with Barry, as though he were to blame."

I slipped the dress over her head, pulled it down, fastened the zipper.

"Though why," she went on, "people want to marry. It's necessary for a woman, of course, but it's really a very unsatisfactory institution. Poor John, I'll miss him greatly. Forty-five years of marriage do become a habit, you know. But sometimes I wonder if it wasn't all for the best. God works in a mysterious way, to be sure. Barry was getting rather tired of having us all around, at least after he married Paula. He felt that she ought to have first place. When you come right down to it, I suppose she should, but I declare we felt like pensioners. Not nice at all. And there was poor sweet Luella. I always thought she had such a soothing influence on Barry."

Ruth brought in the flowers, made some

gushing reference to the fact I'd brought them, looked from her rambling, garrulous mother to me, shrugged her shoulders helplessly and went out.

"I've always loved carnations," Mrs. Hamilton said. "How sweet of you, Sue. You know, I don't believe anyone ever gave me flowers before, except a corsage for my high school graduation, and my father bought that, of course. Do you think it would be all right if I used a very little lipstick or just powder?"

She studied herself in the mirror. "Yes, Luella was so soothing. She was the only one who really understood Barry. When he was working on a book he became very irritable. Very irritable indeed. Except with Paula, of course."

She got up to move the vase of flowers from one end of the table to the other, sniffing them, said, "Pretty things," and came back to look for a black-bordered handkerchief and her black gloves.

"Of course, Barry worked hard, very hard, just as though he had a regular job. No holidays. Nothing. And then he was murdered because of that book. It's so unfair. I've felt that right along." She held my eye, nodding wisely. "Right along I've felt it was most unjust. After all, you can't kill people just because you don't like their books. So unfair."

She trotted across the room to get a black hat, put it on, remembered she didn't need it yet, took it off and stood holding it as though she had forgotten what it was for.

"What was I saying? Oh, unfair. But Barry was so courageous. No matter how people threatened him he just went on writing his books."

"You must have been very proud of them." This seemed to be a safe, noncommittal comment.

"Well, of course I was. They were so successful, if you know what I mean. But, to tell you the truth, I never read them myself. I tried with the first one, but what I really like is a good romance. Something where nothing unpleasant happens and things turn out happily.

"They don't, do they, except in books. Nice books, I mean. Usually people find life rather disappointing. There's poor Tommy wanting to cut loose, as he puts it, from Blanche. Both John and I heard him tell Barry. Well, of course Blanche is a little bit older than he is but I thought she might be a stabilizing influence, you know. But Barry was quite annoyed and said if Tommy wanted out he could get himself a job. It was time he moved out anyhow. If Tommy didn't do something about it, he would because his patience was exhausted. I remember how upset poor John was over the whole thing. They were really shouting. Bad feeling between brothers is such a pity, isn't it? And

206

quarreling with Warren too, as Barry did. Warren was terribly put out and, of course, Ruth was angry with Barry about that.

"You haven't any children, have you, my dear? No, of course not. How absurd of me. Well, it's a gamble. Not at all a logical or satisfactory business, you know, and you simply have no idea what you'll get or how they'll turn out.

"And then the day before he died Barry had that ridiculous disagreement with Paula. I never understood what that was all about. She left the house without explaining anything to anyone and moved over to Mrs. Oliphant's and Barry walked the floor like a caged animal. Here he was done, his book finished, and he should have been so happy. Usually he was quite excited and good-tempered when he had finished, but this time Paula spoiled it all. He was terribly unhappy. Really it was most unreasonable of her.

"Oh," she added hastily, "I'm sure she must really have loved him in her own way or she wouldn't have killed herself." Mrs. Hamilton added in a puzzled tone, "But so extreme of her. I never thought of Paula as an extreme person, if you know what I mean. And that last morning Barry wasn't like himself at all; he looked exhausted but sort of relieved. I think he had talked to Paula. At lunch I said what I needed was some new

207

clothes and he said what he needed was a new job. And I said, 'For heaven's sake you've just finished a book' and he said something queer, 'Othello's occupation's gone.' "

Someone was knocking at the door but Mrs. Hamilton, confused, garrulous, inattentive, did not hear it.

"Come in," I called.

Dexter looked in. "Ready?" he asked gently and helped her to her feet. "It's time for us to be on our way, I think."

"What?" She remembered. Automatically the tears began to roll down her cheeks. Mrs. Hamilton had completed her preparations for the funeral.

II

New York was blazing hot and it was sultry. Fun City was closed in by a film of choking air pollution. On top of everything else, the heap had developed some alarming rattles on the way down. Joe managed somehow to hold on to his good temper but he finally drove into a garage, produced his bill of sale and identification papers, and sold the thing for $75. As it wasn't worth 75¢, I realized there was more Maitland or maybe more Wentworth in his make-up than I had been aware of.

"Haggling," I said in disgust as we left the place and he hailed a cab.

"Watch the pennies and the dollars will take care of themselves," he replied smugly.

The next stop was Cartier's and there he didn't haggle. Only at my insistence would he finally settle for an engagement ring that didn't look like a headlight, though it did, I thought, look remarkably nice on my finger. He made another stop at a luggage shop and came out with a mysterious package, which he refused to relinquish when he checked his hat at the Plaza. It was, I assumed, a surprise present for me. Halfway through lunch he cautiously unwrapped it and showed it to me. Of all things it was a leash.

When we had finished lunch Joe found us some chairs in the lobby. "We're waiting for a friend."

In a few minutes the young reporter, Fischer, came in, looked around, and joined us.

"Well?" Joe asked.

"Well, I've got you transportation home. One of those drive-it-yourself deals. I called every outfit in town. This ought to suit you. It's a nice car."

"Good." Joe glanced at the slip on which Fischer had written the address and pocketed it.

Fischer opened his briefcase and took out the snapshot of Blanche and a sheaf of photostated papers. The whole story of Blanche's arrest in Cairo was there, together with a couple of pictures of her: one taken at the time of her arrest, the other at some official function, wearing the diamond necklace Mrs. Oliphant had mentioned and accompanied by the most repellent man I had ever seen. Silenus, Mrs. Oliphant had said, and that wasn't far off.

His name had been Sylvestrus Bendt, and not much was known about him except that he was rumored to have some link with practically every business, legal and illegal, in the Middle East, and he was closely associated with a disheartening number of politicians.

Mrs. Bendt had called the hotel doctor as soon as she discovered her husband's death. At least that was what she claimed. According to the doctor, the man had been dead for many hours. No conceivable motive for suicide was uncovered and the number of pills he had swallowed wiped out any possibility of accident. The arrest of Mrs. Bendt had caused quite a commotion. She had been married to her horrible husband for some five years. Her background was obscure and no one seemed to know where she came from.

Then the story was dropped for several days and emerged once more when the verdict of suicide was announced. Mrs. Bendt walked out of jail and disappeared into thin air.

Two years later, she arrived in the United States, Fischer had learned from the passport bureau, from Switzerland. During the interval she had apparently salvaged what she could of her husband's confused and unorthodox estate.

Joe grinned at the reporter. "You are holding out on me."

Fischer could not restrain his smile of triumph. "Well, you know people have to sign for these papers. As you said to spare no expense, I found a nice clerk who was willing to work overtime and check back. Two months ago someone asked for the same papers."

"Barry Hamilton?"

"Himself. So we have a motive for her killing him and his wife too, in case Hamilton told her about it, which seems likely, and Luella Matthews, who appears to have been in Hamilton's confidence. But that telephone call to old Mr. Hamilton. I can't figure why she made that, and yet it's the one crime of the lot we're almost certain she committed, as she had tried the same thing that morning in Miss Wales's presence."

"Well," Joe said, "there is work to be done."

"And when," Fischer asked him, "do I stop being your errand boy and get my clearance?"

"Tomorrow. At the very latest the next day. Come up to Stockford in the morning. This thing has to end now."

17

"You know, Sue," Joe said after Fischer had left us, "one thing sticks in my throat. When you found Paula's things there were canceled checks and receipted bills but no letters. Not one single letter."

"They probably never went to Stockford. I know I always wrote to her at the office; she asked me to."

"Which means that someone around the house was a snooper and not above reading other people's mail. Who is your candidate: Blanche or Luella?"

"It was never Paula's home, was it? Not really. It belonged to the Hamiltons and she was the outsider. Joe, do you suppose there would be any mail at her office?"

"Let's find out."

The Webb Publishing Company occupied a floor in a fairly old building on Madison Avenue. There was a closed door marked DEXTER WEBB, PRIVATE, and beyond that an open door marked WEBB PUBLISHING COMPANY. We entered a cheerful reception room with rugs and comfortable chairs, a bowl of fresh flowers on a table that was

212

equipped with ashtrays, the Webb titles in their bright jackets on shelves along the walls, together with a picture of Barry Hamilton looking handsome. Everything about the place was bright and gay and welcoming.

"Paula planned this," I said confidently.

The receptionist was a middle-aged woman with a cultivated voice and a pleasant manner. Her welcoming smile changed when I told her who I was. She pushed back her chair, came out through a little swinging gate from behind her window, calling to someone out of sight to handle the switchboard.

"Oh, Miss Wales, we all loved Mrs. Hamilton! She was so lovely and sweet and incredibly efficient. I don't see how Mr. Webb is going to manage without her and that's a fact. And we miss her horribly. It's as though the sun had gone behind a cloud."

I had been right. It was Paula who had designed the reception room. Before that it had been a dingy affair. Mr. Webb had suggested something modern and functional but Mrs. Hamilton had persuaded him to do it her way.

"Mr. Webb isn't here, you know. He is at the Hamilton house in Connecticut, but we expect him back next week. Mrs. Hamilton's secretary is here though and she would love to see you."

In a few minutes a short stocky girl with a deep summer tan and light intelligent eyes came out to meet us.

"I am Irene Moult, Mrs. Hamilton's secretary." She gave me a firm handshake.

I introduced Joe and she nodded. "I've been reading about you," she said rather dryly. "Would you rather talk here or come back to your sister's office?"

"Her office," I said.

"I'm awfully glad you've come. Mrs. Hamilton's personal mail has been stacking up and I didn't know what to do about it. What with all the trouble at the Hamilton house I didn't like to send it on there, and I couldn't bother Mr. Webb for instructions. He has about all he can manage, so far as I can make out from the papers. I'm glad he could escape some of the mess here: reporters, photographers, everyone you can imagine asking the most impertinent questions. Of course we all sat tight and refused to open our mouths."

We passed a big sunny office with the word *President* on the door and went into a smaller one that had been Paula's. It was cheerful and bright, with Venetian blinds closed against the relentless afternoon sun, a vase of flowers and potted plants. There were two desks, some files, and a few chairs. On one of the desks there was an open typewriter; on the other a stack of unopened mail.

"This is where Mrs. Hamilton worked." Miss Moult touched the desk gently with her

214

hand and went on to her own, waving us to chairs.

I looked over the letters and shoved them into my big handbag. I couldn't read them now.

"I hope I'm not taking up too much of your time."

The girl shook her head. "I'm just going through the motions. There is no place for me here now, as the only possible advance would be to become Mr. Webb's secretary, and she has worked for him ten years. So I've resigned and I'll be job hunting next week."

"I'm sorry."

"I wouldn't have cared to stay on, not without Mrs. Hamilton. She was — something pretty special." The girl blinked tears out of her eyes. She tried to adopt a businesslike tone of detachment. "It's queer, you know. For all she was so arrestingly beautiful that wasn't what struck you most about her. She had a kind of extra sense about books. A sort of instinct. A year ago she tried her best to prevent us from publishing the Worstein book."

"Wow!" Joe exclaimed.

"Wow is right. It was clever, it was plausible, it looked like a big seller but Mrs. Hamilton said no. Usually Mr. Webb followed her advice, but Worstein is part public relations man, part Madison Avenue, and part sideshow barker. He really sold himself to Mr. Webb. Result, that libel suit for half a million dollars." She gave a cynical grin. "Of course the man who brought that suit wanted to protect a reputation he had never had but that's neither here nor there in the courts. So we paid."

"Has it hurt the house much?" Joe asked.

She shrugged. "That kind of publicity never helps a publisher, and having to pay out that kind of money hurts a lot. This is just a small outfit, you know, not over twenty-five titles a year. Of course, if Mr. Hamilton's book on Masters hadn't disappeared, there would be no problem. We would have cleaned up on that."

"Had you seen it?" Joe asked idly.

"Oh, no. No one ever saw one of Mr. Hamilton's scripts until he sent in finished copy, not even Mr. Webb. Oh, I suppose Mrs. Hamilton saw it. She was to edit it, you know. She — they were so much in love. You could almost see it happen the first time they met. Right here in this office. Mr. Webb brought him in. It was just — combustion."

Queer to realize how egotistical we are. Somehow I had thought that my feelings for Joe were something special. I had not realized that the same thing had happened to Paula.

"Of course, Mr. Hamilton was awfully good-looking and he had a kind of charm,

216

elusive sort of thing but unmistakable. All the girls were in a flutter whenever he came in, and the typists were always trailing along the hall trying to get just a glimpse of him. But I must say he wasn't the kind to give them a play. I suppose," she added with detachment, "he didn't need that sort of thing to build his ego."

"What did he need?" Joe asked.

"Someone who would accept him unquestioningly and uncritically at his own valuation."

"And that," Joe commented, "is quite a lot."

"The strangest thing to me," Miss Moult said, "was watching the way Mrs. Hamilton lost all her critical detachment. You know I believe she really gave him all he expected of her."

The woman in the doorway said, "Oh, sorry," and turned away.

"Come in, Jill." Miss Moult performed introductions. Gillian Black was Dexter Webb's secretary, a sandy-haired heavy woman of middle age, wearing for reasons known only to herself a pale pink dress that played havoc with her coloring.

"I'd like to tell you how sorry we are, Miss Wales. How terribly sorry. Everyone here at Webb. Losing Mrs. Hamilton was bad enough. And Mr. Hamilton! The biggest author we ever had. Just everything all at once."

217

Unexpectedly this big, placid-looking woman broke down. Her voice cracked. "They needn't have killed him," she wailed. "That is what is so terrible. They needn't have. Both Mr. and Mrs. Hamilton could be alive today. I hope someone murders Eliot Masters for that. I hope he's ruined forever. Mr. Hamilton wasn't even going to have the book published!"

"What!" Both Joe and Miss Moult spoke at the same time.

The sandy-haired woman nodded. "Mr. Hamilton called here the day he was killed, that very day. Mr. Webb was busy working on budgets and advertising appropriations and didn't want to be disturbed. Mr. Hamilton said it didn't matter. He kind of laughed and said maybe it was just as well. Dex, he always called Mr. Webb Dex, would be upset. I'd better break it to him myself. He said he had come to the decision to destroy the Masters book.

"Well, when the script arrived in the mail today, I nearly fainted. There was a note from Mr. Webb saying the carbon copy had turned up and to send it to the copy editor. But as Mr. Hamilton had decided against publication I'm holding it for Mr. Webb. The Hamiltons aren't answering their telephone — I don't blame the poor things for that — so I can't reach him."

"You mean that Mr. Webb doesn't know

about Hamilton's decision?"

"No, by the time I had got through a lot of dictation and went into his office to have the letters signed he had gone for the day."

"Miss Wales and I are returning to Stockford tonight. Perhaps I had better return the script and explain to him."

"Oh, if you would!" his secretary said gratefully. In a few minutes she came from her own office with a manuscript in a red folder. "You'll be very careful, won't you?"

"I'll guard it with my life. Couldn't you have reached Webb after he left the office that day? I should think a message as important as that —"

"I didn't know where to reach him. He had a date for cocktails and dinner with an author."

"Do you know who it was?"

Miss Black cast an amused look at Paula's secretary. "Willson Palmer."

"Oh, lord!" ejaculated Miss Moult. "What did he want this time? Let me guess. A bigger advance on his next book. Didn't we go into the red on the last one?"

"He thinks the function of a publisher is to keep an author happy, to encourage him."

"Anyone who could discourage Palmer would be performing a public service! But Mr. Webb is so easygoing. And now without Mrs. Hamil—" Miss Moult braked to a sudden halt.

"Know where I can reach this man Palmer?" Joe asked.

"He was supposed to be moving this week," Miss Black said. "I think he called in to give his new address to the receptionist. It isn't in my files yet."

The receptionist had the address and Joe talked to her for a few minutes. When he left, I felt she was looking both thoughtful and startled. I waited until we were outside on the street.

"What on earth are you up to?"

"The only person whose alibi hasn't been checked is Dexter Webb's."

"But that's ridiculous. He lost so much — an author, an income, Paula —"

"Well, we can't pick up that drive-it-your-self car until evening because I told Fischer we'd have dinner in town. So we might as well start moving in literary circles."

Joe had to go to at least four bookshops before he found a copy of a Willson Palmer book. It was on a counter at the back of the shop marked, "One third off."

Mr. Palmer did not as yet have a telephone so we drove in a cab with a noisy radio to the far reaches of the Bronx. Joe was busy leafing through the pages and, to judge by his expression, feeling slightly seasick.

The apartment building was part of one of those housing developments like beehives, each apartment with a balcony that looked out on a dozen other balconies, down at the water towers and smokestacks of lower buildings, and, on a clear day, if any, had an exceptionally dull view of suburban New York.

Somewhere in the apartment a baby was crying. The door was opened by a harassed-looking woman, swathed in a big apron, who was apparently attempting to move furniture.

Yes, she said, she was Mrs. Palmer. From the uneasy flicker of her eyes I had a feeling that she had feared the appearance of a bill collector.

Mr. Palmer was working, she said in a worshipful tone, and was positively not to be disturbed. Whatever the trouble was, she would handle it. Joe introduced himself vaguely as an admirer of Mr. Palmer's work who, being in the neighborhood, had stopped with the hope that perhaps Mr. Palmer could be persuaded to autograph a copy of one of his books.

Apparently Mr. Palmer was not so absorbed in his work as not to hear this, for he came into the room wearing an air of diffident modesty that could not conceal either his pleasure or his intense surprise.

It was typical of Joe that, when he had introduced me, but without explaining my relationship to Paula, and while he was pouring out incredibly fulsome praise, which Palmer accepted without suspicion, he took off his jacket and helped Mrs. Palmer move a heavy chair from one spot to another. It never occurred to Mr. Palmer to lend a hand.

As the baby's cries rose to a scream, Mrs. Palmer muttered an apology and started for the door. Joe suggested that Mr. Palmer join us for a drink somewhere. So we found ourselves in one of those dark cocktail lounges with Willson Palmer.

Before I had had more than a few sips of a dubious martini, Mr. Palmer was halfway through a double Scotch and had launched into speech. He talked about his books, about his working methods, about his inspiration, about the lack of understanding on the part of the publishers who ruthlessly exploited genius, about the heartbreak of poverty, about having to work under noisy conditions, which set his nerves quivering. He did not, as far as I can recollect, seem to worry about Mrs. Palmer's quivering nerves.

He told us about his fascinating neuroses, about writer's block, about his psychoanalyst. I have no objection to psychoanalysts. I don't mind how much people talk to them if it gives them any pleasure. The trouble seems to be that once the bottle is uncorked, the flow never seems to stop.

It wasn't until Palmer was nearly through with his second double Scotch that Joe brought the talk around to the Webb Publishing Company. Mr. Palmer had nothing good to say for the house. Heartless outfit.

What did they care for genius? All they wanted was sales. Might as well be merchandising corsets. Commercial all the way through. Look at the way they all kowtowed to Barry Hamilton. Once he and Hamilton just happened to arrive there at the same time. Which one did Webb see?

Palmer gave a hollow laugh. "Hamilton, of course. Webb came out to meet him and condescended to give me a nod as he took the great man to his private office. He sent out his assistant to talk to me. And she, if you please, was Mrs. Barry Hamilton. Well, I ask you! I knew at once there could be no real rapport between us."

Joe was suitably outraged. "You mean to tell me that Webb never really gave you any personal attention?"

Apparently it occurred to Palmer that this might be a double-edged sword. Ill-treated he might be in the form of suitable advances, but he did not want us to think his work had been looked down on.

"Oh, no. Matter of fact, Webb and I had dinner and drinks a week or so ago, just at the time of the Hamilton murder." The word drinks seemed to strike a spark and, absently, he signaled for a refill without waiting to be asked. "Now that just shows you."

Joe waited politely to be shown.

"Here's an author built up chiefly by all the advertising they give him, by all the publicity he's always giving himself, if you ask me —"

Joe sidestepped neatly. "Webb must have been pretty well shattered by Hamilton's murder."

"Oh, he didn't know about it when I saw him. We talked almost entirely about my new book, though how I am expected to work in a small apartment, with three children, and my wife cooking and getting the place settled and trying to keep the children still, I can't imagine. We've just moved in, you know. Cheaper. Different with Hamilton, of course. He had a big house and he could work in peace and quiet. But do you think Webb could grasp a simple fact like that? I found him adamant." He hunted for another word, couldn't find one. "Adamant. Said he had spent the whole day working on budgets for the new list and he simply couldn't consider the kind of advance I wanted or promise me a full-page ad when the book is published. That's the kind of thing that is ruining this country."

"I suppose you didn't really have time to make your points."

"Oh, we jawed through dinner and sat talking until eight thirty. You'd think he could take longer. But, no, I had had my allotted hour and I should be grateful for that, I suppose. He said he had a script at his apartment that he must read that night. Didn't even take time for more than a single drink before we ate." Palmer's eye caught the waiter's, signaled for a refill.

I looked at Joe in some alarm. Three double Scotches were bad enough. I hoped we would be able to get the man out of the place on his feet after that fourth drink. And it was risky going. Joe looked at his watch and gave an exclamation of dismay, paid the bill and swept Palmer out with him, the latter still talking. We walked the three blocks to his apartment to make sure he got back safely. He staggered inside, forgetting to say good night.

"Well!" I said on a long breath.

"Every cloud has a silver lining. I left that autographed copy of his book in the bar. Pure gain."

Over a quiet dinner at the Pierre he kept me laughing about the lamentable Willson Palmer. We took a taxi to the address Fischer had given Joe and I waited until he drove out in what appeared to be a brand-new Cadillac.

"This," I told him as I got in, "is more like it. This is the style in which I intend to be kept in the future."

He dropped a hand menacingly on the leash, which lay between us on the seat next to the Masters script, but he did not say anything. He spoke only once on the hour and a half drive to Stockford, and something about his expression made me wait until he had solved whatever problem he was struggling with.

"What I can't figure out," he said abruptly, "is what Mr. Hamilton knew or guessed."

18

When he had shut off the motor in front of Mrs. Oliphant's house, Joe said approvingly, "Nice baby." He was referring not to me but to the Cadillac. He leaned over to kiss me in an absent-minded sort of way.

"You get some sleep. I'll have a nightcap and take a look at the notorious Masters script."

"If Barry had only made public what he intended to do," I said bitterly, "he and Paula would be alive today."

"You haven't seen it yet, have you? Don't forget to look through Paula's letters. And, Sue, you're still sure she must have left you a message?"

I nodded.

"Then what did she do with it? You've searched that room of yours?"

"Except for ripping off wallpaper or ripping up floorboards I've searched every inch. It isn't there."

Joe sat unmoving at the wheel. "She had learned about Barry's murder and Mrs. Oliphant, in her robe, had nearly been killed. She knew what the risk was. She was inter-

227

rupted when she tried to talk to you on the telephone. She wanted to get something into your hands and she didn't dare wait. Think, Sue! What could she have done with it?"

But I had thought and thought. I just shook my head in defeat. "Why is Fischer coming up tomorrow?"

"I promised him a story."

"You'll have one for him by then?"

"I hope so. Look here, my darling, you've got to promise me that, whatever the provocation, you won't open your pretty trap. Not to anyone. Not about anything."

"As long as you won't tell me anything there is nothing to say." I was resentful.

He started to take me in his arms and changed his mind, which struck me as a very poor policy.

"Will you lock your door or shall I lock you in?" As there was no choice I agreed that I would lock my door. "I can't afford to take a chance on you. Not with killers like these."

"You mean — there are two of them?"

"That's the way it has to be. Otherwise . . ." He stretched out a hand and flicked me gently on the cheek.

When I had undressed I got into bed and read Paula's letters. Half a dozen were from friends writing about her marriage to Barry, one even saying she had just learned of it and that she was sending a belated wedding present. That jolted me. After all, Paula had been married only three months. In reverse *Hamlet*, the wedding baked meats were being served forth for the funeral.

One letter was from Paula's oldest friend and confidante. Apparently Paula had, under the seal of secrecy, told her of Barry's discovery about Blanche Hamilton.

"In my opinion," the friend had written, "no one would be safe in the house with a woman like that. I think you have every justification for insisting that Barry kick them both out. Especially as you say he doesn't want them around anyhow. It he should ever lose his temper he would probably taunt her with what he knew. And then — look out! Do you suppose that fool Tommy knows what he has let himself in for? In his position I'd never feel easy eating or drinking anything my wife gave me."

There was a letter from a New York lawyer, in answer to one of — I checked back in my mind, it must have been — the day she moved to Mrs. Oliphant's, in regard to a legal separation from her husband. He explained the procedure and suggested that she call his office for an appointment.

Once more I let my reading lamp burn all night. I lay staring at the ceiling. Two murderers, Joe had said. I thought now I could understand that magnificent self-assurance of Blanche Hamilton's. She was a woman who

229

had once got away with murder. She believed she was invulnerable. But — Tommy? His own brother, his own father, his nervous collapse after his father's death, the pounding feet that had followed me along the path in the woods.

Before falling asleep I got up to test the door and make sure it was securely locked.

At breakfast I gave Paula's letters to Joe without comment.

"Don't forget," I reminded him, "to give the Masters script to Dexter. Was it as tough on Masters as people expected it to be?"

"It's as clever a job as I've ever come across," Joe said slowly. "I spent most of the night reading it. And a lot of things are clearing up. It's a vicious job, Sue. All done with kindness. Nothing but implications. Personally, Barry said, he could find no real evidence that Masters had accepted $80,000 from that union leader who went to prison. True, certain things looked dark but no doubt Masters could explain them away. And remember the book was timed to appear at the peak of the campaign so Masters couldn't possibly have marshaled proof of his innocence. There are other juicy bits, including an attempt to suggest that he was secretly married in his early twenties and divorced the girl, leaving her stranded."

"So that's what happened between Paula and Barry. She read the script and gave him

230

twenty-four hours to abandon it. Poor Dexter! It's going to be tough on him when he realizes the book is not publishable."

"Very tough," Joe agreed.

When we went up to see Mrs. Oliphant, we found her for the first time fretful and snappish.

"Dick promised to take this cast off today and to replace it with a lighter one. Now he says he can't come until late this afternoon or tomorrow. I wish he had to lug this thing around! But I suppose he can't help it. His nurse called and said he was rushed off his feet and he had had practically no sleep last night."

"What's happening?" Joe asked. "An epidemic?"

"The funeral. My dears, it must have been ghastly. Somehow word leaked out about the double funeral and there was practically a riot. I had three eyewitness accounts in the afternoon. Mobs of people showed up. They even got into the cemetery and trampled on flowers and graves. It was a disgusting outrage. I'm so glad you were both out of the way. There were quite a few injuries in the crush and that is what is holding Dick up this morning."

"Ghouls," Joe said with unusual heat. "People in mobs aren't like people individually. I distrust all mobs on principle because they represent men at their lowest common

231

denominator, the obedient herd that chants slogans. That's why I abominate every kind of demonstration." It wasn't like Joe to sound off so I realized he was trying to prevent me from thinking of Paula's desecrated grave and fix it on something impersonal.

The little telephone beside Mrs. Oliphant gave a light tinkle and she answered it. The voice at the other end of the line went on and on. In the first pause she said, "Of course I wanted to express my sympathy. Dear John! But at least he had a happy life and the blessing we all long for, of going quickly and painlessly."

Again the voice, now obviously that of Mrs. Hamilton, went on and on. Mrs. Oliphant looked at us in astonishment. "My punch bowl? I would be only too happy. . . . No, not possible at all, unfortunately, I can't get around on this cast. . . . They are both here. . . . I'll ask them."

When she had put down the handset, Mrs. Oliphant stared at us in sheer astonishment. "Brace yourselves, my dears. You are both invited to go to the Hamilton house this afternoon at five for a private — very private — celebration of the engagement of Ruth and Warren King. They plan to be married at once, quietly. And Mrs. Hamilton wishes to know whether I will lend her my punch bowl, though what it's going to be polluted with I can't imagine as that skinflint Warren is to provide the materials for the punch."

"They're getting married at once!" Joe exclaimed.

"I suppose," Mrs. Oliphant said dryly, "Ruth believes in striking while the iron is hot."

"Or King remembers that a wife cannot testify against her husband."

"Against — my dear, what are you talking about?" When Joe made no reply, she turned to me. "You'll find that punch bowl in the corner cupboard in the dining room, if you don't mind delivering it."

Joe took the script of the Masters to the guesthouse and left it on the long worktable with a note explaining why he was returning it. After that he spent most of the day in the village, but he was properly dressed in a white suit when he carried the punch bowl carefully across the lawn late in the afternoon. Somewhat to my surprise it was Mrs. Hamilton herself who admitted us. She appeared to have recuperated rapidly. She had discarded her mourning and she wore a thin summer dress of the drip-dry variety.

"What a pity," she said, when Joe had deposited the punch bowl, "that you were unable to attend the services. So touching. Really most gratifying. And there was such a host of friends. I was quite surprised. I think it must have been in tribute to Barry rather than to poor John and dear Luella. They

233

never seemed to have many friends. Yes, I think it must be attributed to Barry's fame."

My carnations were on a table in the living room and again she thanked me most effusively for thinking of her. The flowers made such a nice bright spot of color. Ruth was in the kitchen preparing canapés. Warren was to make the punch. It seemed only right, even in these trying circumstances, for the young people to have some sort of celebration of their happiness, even though it was strictly family. Perhaps it was best to keep busy at a time like this. Even Dexter was at work, clearing out the guesthouse. He would be going back to New York on Monday and he was not planning to return. Naturally, with Barry gone it couldn't be the same for him.

"Well," she added in a tone of surprise, "of course it won't be the same for any of us. Warren says you aren't going to claim Barry's estate. How sweet of you, Sue dear! I can't pretend that it won't make things easier all the way around. Everything is going to be quite different. Ruth and Warren will probably live here. I think I'll move out to the guesthouse. It's better for a young married couple to live alone. And then," she added shrewdly, "if I have my own establishment I won't be expected to help run this big house. At my age I'm entitled to take things easy."

"Alone?" Joe asked. "What about the Tommy Hamiltons?"

"They are planning to go to South America of all places! Isn't it odd of them?"

"Very unexpected."

"Yes, but perhaps it is for the best." This afternoon Mrs. Hamilton's attitude was one of determined cheerfulness. Far from being crushed by her widowhood, she seemed almost enlivened by it. "As I always say, young people should be by themselves. And really Blanche has been quite unreasonable lately. I can't say but I'll be relieved to have her go. Ever since Tommy and Barry had that quarrel she has been difficult. Actually suspicious. She thought poor John was siding with Barry against Tommy. Then she claimed that someone stole her perfume. Now I ask you! And this time it's her sleeping pills. She's just been going on and on about them because she couldn't sleep last night. And she seems to think Tommy took them, though what he would want with them I can't imagine. He has always slept like a log."

"But if Tommy did take the sleeping pills . . ." I began.

"And what," Tommy demanded, "does that have to do with you? I told you once before, you little witch, to keep your nose out of our affairs."

Joe went into action. He jabbed twice and Tommy hit the floor, an amazed expression on his youthful face.

235

Mrs. Hamilton set up a thin screaming. "In a house of mourning," she wailed. "In a house of mourning."

Joe heaved Tommy to his feet. "There are plenty more where those came from. Keep your filthy tongue off my girl."

He let go and Tommy fell rather than sat on a chair, blinking with bewilderment. He rubbed his elbow where he had cracked it in his fall, felt his stomach gingerly, gave Joe a wary look.

"I didn't see you coming."

"You won't next time either."

"Now, boys," Mrs. Hamilton twittered as she hurried out of the room, away from trouble. Considerably to my surprise both men broke out laughing.

Feeling that the tension had eased and that he was safe, Tommy said with an injured air, "What was the idea of knocking me around?"

"That's just the first installment for hitting Sue."

"I don't know what you mean." Tommy looked genuinely astonished. "Why should I do a thing like that?"

"Because my girl talks too much. She told you there was a murderer in this house and she warned you not to let your wife scare the living daylight out of your father again."

Blanche barged in, stabbing each of us with a look. "I could hear you shouting clear upstairs. I've come to warn you, Maitland, to get your hooks out of Tommy." At first I thought it was just the possessiveness of a greedy woman defending her property; then I realized that she was actually in love with her worthless young husband, that she would defend him like a lioness defending her cub.

"I understand you are planning to go to South America."

"What's that to you?"

"You started packing when you found out that we were staying with Mrs. Oliphant. What was wrong, Mrs. Hamilton? Were you afraid of that snapshot she took, that you'd find yourself involved in murder — again?"

"I'm not afraid of anything."

"Except losing Tommy."

"Tommy has absolute faith in me," she said with the arrogance that distinguished her.

"I wonder. He has certainly been covering for you. He must have known you lied about taking sleeping pills when Barry was murdered; lied about looking for a book when Luella was strangled. He's been doing his best to keep you in the clear. And that's probably the only overtime work he has ever done in his life."

Tommy lifted his chin with the virtuous air of Prince Hal declaring that he will astonish the world by his future amendment. "That's a damned insulting thing to say. A man who wouldn't defend his own wife —"

"His meal ticket," Joe said brutally. "What

237

do you know about this woman, Tommy? Do you know her husband died of an overdose of sleeping pills in Cairo and that she bribed her way out of a murder charge? Hadn't you better start wondering what is in your food and drink? Once a poisoner, you know."

"There's not a word of truth in that!"

"Barry knew all about it. Luella knew too, I think. Barry got rather fed up with the situation, didn't he? When you wanted him to help you get rid of Blanche and at the same time to support you, he turned you down flat."

Blanche drew in her breath with a hiss. "He never did! Tommy never wanted —"

"I wonder," Joe said dreamily, "what Barry would have done if he had lived. I suggest your father tried to intervene, and asked Barry to give you enough money to live on — by yourself. It was a mistake for him to intervene, wasn't it, Tommy? Because he was silenced permanently."

"My father had a heart attack."

"He did indeed. It was brought about by an anonymous telephone call telling him there would be one more death. And there was. His. You've been afraid of that all along, haven't you? But you dodged facing the truth."

Tommy did not seem to age; he seemed to wither like fruit left too long unpicked. "That would be murder."

238

"That was murder."

"Tommy!" Blanche said. "Tommy, don't believe him. Don't believe him, Tommy."

"I'm going to call the hospital and see whether the operators will recognize your voice," Joe said.

Blanche flung out her hand in a gesture that was a dead giveaway.

"You!" Tommy said. "You killed the old man." He stood swaying, hanging on to his chair. "God! He was so harmless. Why did you do it, Blanche?"

19

"No, you don't, Tommy dear," Blanche said. "You aren't going to push this thing off on me. You've been worth a lot to me but not that much. I was willing to cover for you up to a point but I won't take a murder rap for you. You didn't chase Sue through the woods because she said something about me; you went after her because she said there was a murderer in this house. And you know who it is, don't you? You know better than anyone."

Aware that she had lost Tommy irretrievably, she cut her losses and she was selling him right down the river without a moment's compunction.

Tommy simply gaped at her, too stunned to be able to summon up any response.

"Okay," Joe said wearily, "let me guess. You both saw Barry's dead body before Luella discovered it, didn't you?"

Tommy stared at his shoes.

"Barry sent for me," Blanche said. "He dared to send for me. And I'm not used to being given orders, I can tell you that. He said he had found out about the business in Cairo. Not that there was anything in it,

240

mind, but he was going to hold it over my head if I didn't clear out and give Tommy a divorce.

"I didn't know how Tommy was going to take it, hearing about that business, I mean. Not that he would believe it, but if he started worrying about sleeping pills and all like that — well, I was mad clear through. And Barry sat looking at me, you know the way he did, that smile on his face. I could have —" She checked herself.

"Well, the matter sort of hung fire until he could finish that damned book. All that last week Barry was in a foul temper. He raised hell with everyone, Warren and Ruth and Tommy. And then, the day before he died, Paula moved out. I don't know what happened that last morning. He was — different."

"And at lunch," I put in, "he said 'Othello's occupation's gone.' "

"Yeah. Something like that. Anyhow, he said he wanted to see Tommy in his study later on. You'd think he was God Almighty the way he ordered people around. Well, I waited until I couldn't stand it. I had to know what he — what Tommy — so I went around to the outside door of the study and looked in. Barry was lying on the floor, his head a mess, and Tommy was standing beside the desk. The door of the hall was open and I could see the old man in the

241

dining room polishing a loving cup.

"Well, I got the hell out of there and took a sleeping pill. I couldn't afford to be involved in another murder. Then when the thing turned out to be a political job, I thought maybe Tommy had just happened to find Barry after he was killed, that he'd had nothing to do with it but, like the rest of the Hamiltons, didn't want to get involved."

"I did find him dead." Tommy said earnestly, "I swear to God. He was dead when I went in there."

"And why didn't you call the police? Raise an outcry?"

"I headed for the downstairs lavatory and was sick. When I got over that Luella was screaming and —"

Joe looked him over judicially. "You really are a little beauty, Tommy. I suppose that's when your father saw you."

Tommy flushed painfully and then his color faded. "If he saw me, he must have died thinking I was a murderer."

"That's just about the size of it. But not right away. In the beginning I think he shared the family ability to dodge anything he didn't want to face. He grabbed at the idea of a political crime. But when Luella was strangled — where were you then?"

"Asleep," Tommy said, not even expecting us to believe him.

Blanche snorted. "Luella made that crack

at dinner, so I was afraid Barry had left some records in his files. I went down to see for myself. I intended to use the outside door but I saw the old man out on the lawn, staring in. So I went down the hall. Tommy shot out of the study to the dining room where he poured himself a slug of brandy. And there was Luella. Well, I thought he had beat me to it — I mean at looking at the files — but before I could check on them Ruth came in, and I screamed as though I had just seen the body. I thought Tommy had lost his head," for a moment her mouth twitched, "protecting his meal ticket, as you said. The old man — no telling what he saw, what he might think he ought to do about it — I wanted to help Tommy out."

Mrs. Hamilton bustled into the room, having apparently forgotten the violence that had driven her away, and insensitive to the tension she found. She was followed by Dexter who was carrying a tray of glasses. Behind him came Ruth with a platter of canapés and Warren with the punch bowl.

"Do thank Mrs. Oliphant for lending us the punch bowl," Mrs. Hamilton said, "and thank her again for her flowers and her kind letter of sympathy. Truly touching, and so much appreciated. Please tell her —"

For a moment the room whirled around me and then steadied. Joe was beside me, gripping my arm.

"What's wrong?"

"That message Paula left me. I know where it is."

"A message?" Mrs. Hamilton said vaguely.

I could see that Joe wanted to choke me but he rose manfully to the occasion. Under those most unlikely circumstances he even managed to engender a certain spurious gaiety into the occasion. It was he who offered a toast to the happy couple, he who took the plate of canapés from Ruth and passed it, he who cleared a spot for them on the coffee table near the couch on which I was sitting.

Tommy was making a desperate attempt to rally himself for the occasion but he was unable to talk. Except for Warren, unexpectedly expansive, a man who had been reprieved, Joe had little help, not even from me. I was afraid of saying the wrong thing.

"Find the script?" Joe asked.

"Yes, but why the hell did you bring it back?" Dexter demanded in irritation. "I told you time was of the essence. If we don't get the book distributed during the campaign it will be as dead as a burned-out firecracker."

"But your secretary told me Barry had decided against publication."

Dexter spilled the punch with which he was refilling our glasses. "Oh, my God! That really puts the lid on."

"What are you going to do?"

"I haven't the foggiest idea," he confessed. "I'll get at the script tonight and see what it's all about. But what in the name of God made him change his mind?"

I started to speak and Joe bent over me, whispering, "Yawn, baby, yawn."

I looked up to see that he was deadly serious. There was a faint shine of perspiration on his face. I yawned. Apologized. Yawned again.

Joe laughed in embarrassment. "I'm terribly sorry to break this up but my girl seems to be out on her feet." He took my arm and steered me out. "Stagger just a bit," he breathed in my ear, and put his arm around me.

When we were inside the Oliphant house I said indignantly, "Why on earth did you want me to act as though I were tight?"

"Not tight. Doped." Then I saw Fischer, Lieutenant Graby, and Sergeant Knight waiting in the living room. To my surprise Joe handed a punch glass to Graby.

"What's that?"

"Another attempted murder. At least that's my guess. Probably one of the barbiturates. Blanche Hamilton's sleeping pills are missing."

"You mean that punch was doped?" I demanded.

"I think your glass was. That's why I bustled around so helpfully clearing the coffee

245

table. I exchanged glasses with you."

"You didn't drink mine?" I was horrified.

"No, I set it outside the window and picked it up when I left."

"Warren?" I was bewildered. "He made the punch. But why?"

"Because you told everyone in loud and ringing tones that you knew where Paula's message was."

"Well, I'd just thought of it."

Dr. Ames came in. "There's another police car outside. For God's sake, what is happening now?"

Joe explained about the punch and the doctor said he would have it analyzed.

"Let's go," Joe said, and he went out followed by the two policemen and Fischer who seemed to have blind faith that he knew what he was doing.

"Where are they going?" Dr. Ames asked.

"I think they are going to catch a murderer," I said through dry lips.

"Who?"

"I don't know."

The doctor looked at me sharply. "I was counting on your help with this cast."

"You'll get it."

While he worked, cutting off Mrs. Oliphant's heavy cast, I told them both about the scene at the Hamilton house. "It was unspeakable. The moment when Tommy had to face the fact that his wife was responsible for

246

his father's death was horrible. And she knew she'd lost him so she didn't waste a minute in practically accusing him of the murders. And then someone doped my punch glass. At least, Joe thinks so."

Mrs. Oliphant gave a little exclamation of relief when the two heavy pieces had been laid to one side. I helped with the work of wrapping the lighter cast, then, as the doctor reached for the old one I said, "Wait!"

I carried the pieces to the window. There, imbedded in the plaster were two small pieces of paper. With the doctor peering over my shoulder I deciphered them with some difficulty as the paper was wrinkled and discolored and in some places almost illegible.

At last Dr. Ames said, "So that's it! Well, I'll be damned."

I focused Mrs. Oliphant's binoculars, looking for Joe and the other men, saw them moving cautiously behind the hedge. Then there was a flicker of movement as someone darted behind the guesthouse toward the woods path. There was a flash as Fischer took a picture. I saw the white shocked face of Dexter Webb.

II

When I had covered the distance between Mrs. Oliphant's house and the guesthouse

247

Dexter was saying, "I tell you this stuff was planted on me, as Luella's necklace was planted. You're damned right I wanted to get rid of it."

"This stuff" was two bottles, one a black perfume bottle with a crystal stopper, the other a small medicine bottle.

"Who do you think would plant it on you?" Graby asked.

"Blanche, of course," Dexter said in surprise. "These belong to her. Maitland can tell you he found Luella's necklace in my room and Sue smelled Blanche's perfume. You know, by the way, don't you, that Blanche and Tommy are planning to clear out, to go to South America?"

"They were," Graby said. "I think I can change their minds for them. They would be wise to stick around for a while."

Dexter looked questioningly at the lieutenant. "So it was Blanche then. I had my eye on Warren."

"Blanche Hamilton probably put through the telephone call that killed her father-in-law," Graby said. "But I'm not sure we could prove intent, even if we got a definite identification of her voice."

"Do you mean," Dexter said incredulously, "that you are going to let Barry's killer get away with it?"

"Oh, no," Graby said, "not at all. I am taking you in for questioning about the mur-

248

ders of Barry Hamilton, Paula Hamilton, and Luella Matthews." Sergeant Knight had loomed up at his side.

Dexter stood stock-still. "Why in the name of God," he asked, "would I murder Barry?"

"I know why," I said.

Joe whirled around. "I told you to keep out —" The meaning of my words registered. "You found it!"

"I found it. Paula put it in Mrs. Oliphant's cast. She was frightened and she didn't know how much time she had."

"What is it?"

"Come and see."

While Lieutenant Graby and the sergeant led the way, Dexter between them, dead white but head high, I followed between Fischer and Joe.

For the first time Mrs. Oliphant was downstairs, sitting on the couch. Beside her were the two heavy pieces of her plaster cast. Behind her stood the young trooper named Wellcome, who had helped in our search for the missing script.

As the little procession trooped into her living room Mrs. Oliphant looked quickly from face to face. She was very pale. "Dr. Ames asked me to tell you that he'll call as soon as he has analyzed that glass of punch."

Dexter seemed to brace himself and then, at a gesture from the sergeant, he sat beside him on the love seat.

249

"Well, Miss Wales?" Graby asked.

"Just a few minutes after Barry was murdered," I said, "Mrs. Oliphant was thrown down the stairs in mistake for Paula and broke her leg. Paula being Paula helped Dr. Ames with the cast. She," I swallowed, "must have been terrified. She knew about Barry. She guessed about herself. She was desperate to get some information to me. So she hid it in the cast."

"Why didn't she tell the doctor?"

Knowing Paula, I think she had to be sure before she accused anyone. She always believed the best of people until she had the truth thrust on her. But she had in her hands proof of the motive for Barry's murder. After hiding it she tried to call me, probably from the phone on the Hamilton terrace. She was stopped before she could tell me where she had left that message. Stopped forever."

I showed him the cast, showed him the stained, wrinkled papers embedded in it. Graby bent over them, struggling to make them out.

"Can you figure them out?" he asked. "We'll take them to headquarters. They have men who —"

"I can read them." I read aloud:

"This is to acknowledge that I am holding $250,000 in bearer bonds to be paid to Barry Hamilton on completion of his book

250

on Eliot Masters." It was signed Dexter Webb.

The other was in Paula's big scrawl: "For my sister, Sue Wales: Sue precious, I don't know what else to do. If anything happens to me before the cast is removed, Dexter will have killed me as he killed Barry. In that case, you'll have to carry on." That one I deliberately read aloud in Paula's high sweet voice, watching Dexter's face.

"Oh, God!" The words seemed to be wrenched out of him.

20

Joe came back from the telephone. "He's not talking, of course. He'd be a fool to."

"But that alibi of his, Joe."

He shook his head. "Webb was supposed to be in his office all afternoon working on budgets and advertising appropriations. Then he was to have cocktails and dinner with Willson Palmer. But his phone and his secretary's are on the same line. I checked that with the operator. He must have heard Barry's call and his decision not to publish. So he hired a drive-it-yourself car, the one we drove up here, incidentally. Fischer got a positive identification. He was back in New York in time to meet Palmer for dinner. Remember that Palmer said he had had his allowed hour and that Webb left him at eight thirty, giving Webb an hour and a half to drive back to New York after he killed Paula. But what you are crying about, Niobe, I'm damned if I can see."

"He seemed so nice. When did you guess? When we were in New York?"

Joe shook his head. "In a way I had a kind of hunch about him when he showed up at the inn and quoted that line of Webster's: 'Cover her face; mine eyes dazzle; she died young.' If you remember, it was the man who incited the murder of the Duchess of Malfi who spoke that line. It just stuck in my mind. And then, from the beginning, he kept hammering home the fact that he had the most to lose by Barry's death. And he was the first one to show an interest in you while, if you were right, the murderer believed Paula had got a message to you."

Actually, the thing went back to that streak of malice in Barry Hamilton, which made him misuse his great talent and write books that tore reputations to tatters. When Eliot Masters began to climb steadily to the top as contender for the presidency, something had to be done to stop him. Who thought of using Hamilton for the job, who supplied the $250,000 in bearer bonds, no one knew. It was unlikely they would ever know. No one would dare claim the money, which, of course, gave Webb a margin of safety. Even if there were strong suspicions against him nothing could ever be said.

Apparently the approach had been made to Dexter Webb, because his house was small and he had taken a terrific financial beating with the $500,000 Worstein libel suit. Presumably Barry had agreed to do the job less for the extra money than for the sheer amusement he got out of the sense of power

253

derived from destroying the career of a bigger man than himself.

Then he finished the book and turned it over to Paula to edit. Up to that point she had been profoundly in love with him and he with her. But she recognized the book for what it was. She broke with him, giving him twenty-four hours to make up his mind. And as she was a woman who took swift action, she wrote to a lawyer about a legal separation, moved next door until Barry could come to a decision, and changed her will.

Barry had put months of labor into the book and it was practically guaranteed a financial success. It was a terrible decision for him to make, but his father had been right. In the long run, his love for Paula was stronger than his desire to publish. He had obviously turned over to her Webb's receipt for the bearer bonds, announced at lunch that "Othello's occupation's gone," and called the office to announce his decision.

Webb must have been in a state of panic. The Masters book would undoubtedly have outsold anything Barry had ever done. Webb could not afford to lose it. But, worst of all, he had dipped into the bonds to help pay off the law suit and he knew Barry well enough to realize that he would never let him get away with that.

I broke in to ask how Joe knew about the bearer bonds.

"He didn't have any other way of paying the libel. I've had people checking the Webb Publishing Company finances back and forth. He didn't have that kind of money."

Well, he had raced out to talk it over with Barry, to try to persuade him to change his mind, but he had found him adamant. So he had smashed him over the head and he took the script as a red herring. Eventually he intended to produce the carbon copy and publish it. But Barry saw him in the mirror. What Joe believed Luella had overheard was Barry saying, "It wouldn't do you any good. I've told Paula. So don't —" But it was too late. Once Barry knew of his intention Dexter had to go through with it. And he still had a chance of winning the jackpot. Except for Paula.

Dexter loved Paula but he loved his own skin more. He slipped over to the Oliphant house and attempted to strike her down, learned that he had made a mistake, watched for her, caught her at the telephone, and drowned her.

"He'd have got away with it," Joe said, "and Eliot Masters would have a black mark for life if you hadn't been so sure that Paula had not killed herself. And then today you piped up and said you knew where she had left the message for you. Of course, that's why he tried to dope you with the sleeping pills he had stolen from Blanche. I was on

255

the lookout from the moment I heard they were missing. It was his second attempt, you know. He tried once before on the path through the woods."

"But why kill Luella?"

"Judging by what she said about rebuilding her life, the presence of her necklace in the guesthouse, and Blanche's comments, I'd gather Dexter was having a love affair with her. She knew so much about Barry's affairs that she was always a danger. Then he slipped up and took you for a ride and she nearly blew her top. So he decided to silence her permanently."

"We've got that doped glass of punch Dexter served Sue, but no way of proving he doped it or that it was intended for her. We have the receipt in the cast and Paula's message, but there's no trace of the bonds and Paula was assumed to die while of unsound mind. We've a nice picture of Dexter attempting to bury the two incriminating bottles but we can't prove that they were not planted on him. We can blow up his alibi and prove he hired a drive-it-yourself car and put exactly 120 miles on the speedometer during the hours when Barry and Paula were killed. But — we can't prove he killed Barry. We can't prove he killed Paula. We can't prove he killed Luella."

After a while I said, "Then I smelled perfume in the guesthouse because Barry had

256

been handling the bottle."

Joe nodded.

"So?" I asked.

"So," Joe said, "according to Lieutenant Graby there is an excellent chance that in the long run Dexter Webb can get out of this and that Blanche Hamilton will take the rap for the whole thing. And Tommy, as her presumed heir, probably wouldn't do a thing to stop it.

"It's rather ironical, isn't it, that Blanche was cleared of the murder she probably committed, that she can't be brought to trial for the death of John Hamilton for which she is certainly responsible, but that she may get a first-degree sentence for three murders of which she is innocent?"

"But that couldn't possibly happen, could it?"

"A smart lawyer, leaking the information of her first husband's death and on the basis of 'once a killer, always a killer,' could raise enough doubt of Webb's guilt to throw out the case against him and provide a nice case against the lady."

"That," I said, "is according to Lieutenant Graby. But according to Joe Maitland —"

"Joe Maitland," he said, "believes in the influence of a free press. This is going to be Fischer's finest hour."

II

Fischer got the scoop of his life. As no one was sure how the cat would jump he was caution itself. But he got a story, carefully written, with two pictures, one of Dexter trying to bury the two incriminating bottles, one a blown-up job of the receipt and Paula's note to me.

"Where," he concluded, "are the bearer bonds which paid for the anti-Masters book?"

It paid off in spades. Within twelve hours the attorney in the Worstein case appeared, doing his duty as a citizen, he claimed, and incidentally reminding the public that he had been the man to win one of the biggest libel suits on record. Webb, he declared, had turned over $200,000 in bearer bonds in part payment of the libel suit.

Eliot Masters, of whom everyone had been believing the worst, was suddenly regarded as an angel of light. It was surprising to discover how many people now claimed they had never believed a word against him. It was like trying to find an avowed Nazi in Germany after the war.

The queerest effect of the whole business, to me at least, was the enormous boom in Barry Hamilton's books. The early ones, now out of print, were quickly reprinted to meet the demand. Actually the unprecedented

Hamilton sales saved the Webb Publishing Company from bankruptcy and it was bought up by an enterprising young publisher.

The case never came to trial, of course. Three days after the disclosures about the book and Webb's misuse of the bearer bonds came to light, he hanged himself in his cell. With his charm and his good looks there is a chance he might have drawn a "not guilty" verdict, particularly if there were women on the jury. At any rate, he didn't think it was worth the gamble. He was discredited, stripped of honor, and he had murdered three people. He had, I think, really loved Paula. I wonder how much she haunted him at the last.

Mrs. Oliphant asked Joe and me to be married from her house but we never wanted to see Stockford again. Instead we were married in the rose garden at Joe's house without a single reporter knowing about it.

We planned a three-month trip abroad but that afternoon the telephone rang. Eliot Masters was calling. His voice was so loud and jubilant that Joe had to hold the phone away from his ear.

"I'm entering the primaries. Look here, Maitland, I need you. Will you help with the campaign?"

Joe put his arm around me, holding me close. "I have other plans."

"You," I told him, "are going to do some

honest work for a change."

Joe laughed. "I'll call you later," he promised. "About a month later."

Joe and the Scandinavian countries, Joe and Holland, Joe and Spain, and Joe almost made me forget the Hamilton tragedies until we returned to be met by a barrage of newsmen. Eliot Masters had not been backward about giving credit where credit was due, a rare thing in a politician. I left Joe to deal with the press; I had begun to think he could deal with anything. Right now he is immersed in the presidential campaign and having the time of his life.

Yesterday I got a long letter from Mrs. Hamilton of all people. Ruth and Warren are married and they have taken over the Hamilton house. She herself has moved out to the guesthouse. Blanche got a Reno divorce and disappeared. Tommy is being assiduous in his attentions to a wealthy widow who came to the village as a summer visitor and decided to settle there.

"I think," Mrs. Hamilton wrote, "she should be a stabilizing influence for Tommy. She's a little bit older, you know."

We hope you have enjoyed this Large Print book. Other G.K. Hall & Co. or Chivers Press Large Print books are available at your library or directly from the publishers.

For more information about current and upcoming titles, please call or write, without obligation, to:

G.K. Hall & Co.
P.O. Box 159
Thorndike, Maine 04986 USA
Tel. (800) 257-5157

OR

Chivers Press Limited
Windsor Bridge Road
Bath BA2 3AX
England
Tel. (0225) 335336

All our Large Print titles are designed for easy reading, and all our books are made to last.